Also By H.D. Daughrity

<u>*Novels*</u>

Knock Knock

Tales My Grandmother Told Me

Echoes of the Dead: Collected Hauntings

<u>*Anthology Contributions (under Heather Miller)*</u>

These Lingering Shadows

The Horror Zine Magazine Fall, 2022

Into the Forest: Tales of the Baba Yaga

Tales from the Monoverse

Head Blown: Extreme Horror Stories

The Depths Unleashed, Volume One

The Horror Collection: Creature Feature Edition

Deathrealm: Spirits

KNOCK KNOCK

H.D. Daughrity

Published by Parlor Ghost Press, an imprint of Watertower Hill Publishing, LLC.

Copyright © 2023 Parlor Ghost Press, LLC
www.parlorghostpress.com

Cover by Christy Aldridge, Grim Poppy Design.
Copyright © 2023 Parlor Ghost Press, LLC

Author's Note
All character and names in this book are fictional and are not designed, patterned after, nor descriptive of any person, living or deceased.
Any similarities to people, living or deceased is purely by coincidence.

Library of Congress Control Number:

Trade Paperback ISBN: 979-8-9855562-4-7

For Grandma Nan

Who taught me to love the things that go bump in the night.

PROLOGUE

Hillview Paranormal Investigation Team

The November evening was freezing.

Just one week ago the trees had been full of brilliantly colored leaves, but a week of rain and winds had left nothing but bare, dark branches against an orange sky.

From their vantage point at the top of the hill, the investigation team watched as the glowing orb of the sun sank below the horizon, tinting the world in shades of fire.

Shifting the straps of the heavy bag he was carrying, Jackson Green, the team's official tech expert, hurried the three girls ahead of him up the cracked sidewalk and onto the wide front porch of the Victorian monstrosity that sat atop the hill.

The boards creaked under their weight; drifts of dead leaves trapped between the porch railings crunched beneath their boots.

Teresa Rutledge, self-appointed leader of the Hilldale Paranormal Research Team, pulled a set of keys from her bag.

"So, no welcoming committee here, huh?" Carrie Jameson, the youngest of the group, asked.

Her eyes scanned the dark windows, heavy drapes closed against prying eyes, the fast-fading sky reflected against their opaque surface.

"Nope." Melissa Newark brought up the rear, holding a clipboard and fighting against the wind to keep the papers on it flattened down.

"Older lady who owns it didn't want to see us. Cranky old bird, honestly. Lives in town now, I guess. Haven't actually met her in person. Just a couple of phone calls, and she dropped off the keys in the mail slot yesterday."

"We don't need to see the owner. We only need to see the ghosts." Teresa spoke over her shoulder as she pushed against the front door. It swung soundlessly open.

The house was in darkness, a window in a room at the back, visible down a long, straight hallway just in front of them, letting in the last pink-purple glow of twilight.

Teresa pulled a flashlight from her bag, shined it around a bit.

"Ah-ha!" she cried, reaching for the wall and flicking a switch.

"Let there be light!"

It took half an hour for the team to set up their equipment, claiming the large room at the back of the house – the kitchen – as their base of operations, spreading laptops and other electronics across the scarred surface of an old table, cords running across and down to the power strips on the floor like tangled snakes.

The large case with all their handheld devices was opened, and the team divided up the gadgets – handheld cameras, tiny digital recorders, infrared thermometers.

The girls ranged around the downstairs rooms, setting up three static video cameras while Jackson sat at the command center watching the laptop screens and telling them to move their cameras up or down or left or right to get the perfect angles.

The last dying bit of light was gone from the sky when they finished setting up, cold dark pressing against the windows and the wind whistling down through the long-abandoned chimneys.

"Alright, team," said Teresa.

"Tonight we are investigating the downstairs only. Repeat, downstairs only. All reported phenomena are located in the downstairs rooms."

All eyes were on her as she continued giving orders.

"Girls let's start at the front of the house and work our way back. Jackson, stand by here at base command. Let's go, team," Teresa said adamantly.

The other team members rolled their eyes at Teresa's ridiculous attempt at a commanding voice. This was only their fourth case, and they were already getting sick of her.

But the team had been her idea, and it was her money that bought most of the equipment and besides, it wasn't like there was much else interesting to do in Hillview, Missouri.

Teresa led the other two girls slowly down the hallway, their way lit only by the dim light of the one small bulb they'd left on over the kitchen sink. Each girl gripped her video recorder tightly, filming the faded wallpaper of the hallway, the dim shadowy spaces beyond the few doors that opened off of it.

Teresa stopped without warning, causing Melissa to bump into her, and Carrie to bump into her.

"I almost forgot," Teresa whispered, pointing her camera at a small dark shape jutting out from the wall.

She angled her flashlight in the same direction, revealing an old circular thermostat.

"One of the complaints here is that the thermostat changes on its own. They set it to one thing, and when they come back it's gone up or down several degrees on its own."

She motioned for Melissa to zoom in on the thermostat with her camera to record the temperature setting.

"We'll check it throughout the night to see if anything happens."

The girls made their way into the front room, an old-fashioned parlor: a marble fireplace on the wall opposite the doorway, heavy furniture with carved wood along the backs and arms and tufted velvet cushions.

"Let's get settled in here, ladies," Teresa said.

She sat down on the sofa near the fireplace. Melissa took up her post, leaning against the mantel. Carrie slid down and sat on the floor, leaning back against the doorframe.

They all knew the drill. They would sit in silence for a while, listening the sounds of the old house, reaching out with their subconscious, getting used to the house and letting it get used to them.

After what she deemed an acceptable length of silence, Teresa cleared her throat and suggested that they begin taking readings and attempting EVP sessions.

Carrie turned on her handheld thermometer and began scanning the room, pointing the device at walls and tables and chairs and…

"Whoa," she breathed.

Immediately Teresa was at her side, pressing in close to see what the thermometer showed on its dim electronic display.

"Watch this," Carrie said, swinging the thermometer to the left.

The display read sixty-six degrees. She swung it slowly toward the right, the temperature fluctuating in tiny spikes and dips – a tenth of a degree or two up or down.

Teresa frowned. Totally normal.

But then Carrie swept the thermometer just a little further to the right, pointing it directly at the armchair that sat by the front window. The display suddenly read sixty-four degrees, sixty-one, fifty-eight, finally settling at fifty-five degrees.

"Holy crap," Teresa breathed, recording the whole thing as she instructed Carrie to do it again.

As before, the display showed a regular sixty-six degrees until it hit the chair, where it dropped again. Fifty-five degrees.

Melissa had come to watch, and she eyed the chair with a cautious curiosity.

"Now, wait, guys. We have to be thorough here. Maybe it's just colder there because the chair is in front of that window. There might be a draft of cold air seeping in around it."

Carrie stood up from her crouch and approached the chair, stopping halfway across the room. She pointed the thermometer at the window behind the chair, at the thick drapes hiding the outside world from view. It was slightly colder there - sixty-four degrees – but not as cold as the chair itself.

"Give me that," Teresa whispered, taking the thermometer from Carrie's hand.

With her camera trained on the display, she pointed it at the window herself. Sixty-four degrees. She edged closer to the wall and pointed the thermometer at the small bit of empty space between the chair and the window.

Sixty-five degrees. She angled it and pointed at the back of the chair. Still sixty-five degrees.

She walked around, stopping three feet in front of the chair and pointed it at the seat cushion. The temperature dropped quickly. Fifty-five degrees.

"Teresa?" Carrie's voice was quiet, shaking. "Does that mean… is there… is there a ghost… in that chair?"

Teresa's heart pounded hard in her chest. This was the coolest thing she'd ever seen.

"Melissa. Get out your digital recorder. Let's do EVPs."

The three girls settled themselves onto the floor, careful not to lean against walls or furniture that might creak or groan while they were recording. Melissa switched on the recorder.

"EVP session. Carver house. Front room. Melissa, Teresa, and Carrie speaking." She paused a moment, breathing deeply, then went on.

"We are speaking to any spirits who may be here with us. My name is Melissa. These are my friends, Teresa and Carrie. We mean you no harm. We only wish to speak with you. Is there anyone here?"

They waited in silence. In her head, Teresa counted to ten before continuing.

"We would like to communicate with you. Can you tell us your name?"

One, two, three...

"Can you tell us what year it is?"

One, two, three...

"Is there a message you'd like to share with us, or that you'd like us to share with someone else for you? Please tell us now."

One, two, three...

Melissa looked at Teresa and raised her eyebrows. Teresa shook her head, pressing her finger against her lips to signal silence. She closed her eyes and listened. The other two girls did the same. They waited.

Nothing happened.

Teresa sighed. "Come on, let's go back to base and listen to that recording. Maybe we'll hear something on the playback."

They all shuffled back to the kitchen, checking the thermostat on the way – still set to sixty-five degrees – and took turns listening to the EVP through the one set of headphones they all shared.

"I don't hear anything."

"Me neither."

"Nothing. Jackson, did you hear anything?"

"Nope. Just you three," Jackson said.

"Well," Teresa announced, "I'm going back to check that cold spot again."

Jackson stood and stretched. "I'll come with you. Need to get my circulation going a bit."

Ten minutes later, they were back.

"Nothing. The damn chair is the same temperature as everything else again!"

Teresa threw the thermometer down on the table with a huff. Jackson leaned against the counter and folded his arms across his chest.

"Are you girls sure you were using that thing the right way? User error and all that." He raised his eyebrows and grinned.

Teresa glared at him. "Listen, Jackson…"

They all froze.

A noise from the hallway. A faint thump. Another. Another.

Footsteps, Teresa mouthed silently, raising her camera to point down the hall.

Carrie shrunk back against the wall; eyes wide.

The noises stopped. The team listened hard in the silence, no one daring to breathe.

The noises began again. Teresa counted in her head: one thump, two thumps, three, four, five….

The noise stopped again.

The only movement was Carrie's huge eyes, darting back and forth from Teresa's face to Melissa's to Jackson's and back again, her watching them as they watched the hallway.

Carrie's breath suddenly caught in her throat. She felt cold all over, like someone was shooting a needle full of icy water straight into her veins. Her stomach cramped, her head began to hurt, a pounding darkness seeped into her vision and made the room tilt in front of her.

Carrie's body slid to the floor with thud. The others rushed to her, Teresa checking her pulse as Jackson laid her down flat on the floor. Melissa brushed the hair from Carrie's face but kept her own eyes locked on the dark hallway just beyond.

"Poor kid," Teresa said, laying Carrie's arm down gently.

"Scared her so bad she passed right out." She patted Carrie's face a few times, firmly but gently, till Carrie let out a soft moan and turned her head away.

"Maybe she should stay here with Jackson, sit for a while, drink some water," Melissa suggested.

Teresa looked at Carrie pushing herself upright against the wall, and nodded once, decisively.

"Yes. I think that would be wise."

So, Jackson pulled a second chair around and helped Carrie into it. Together they hunched over the laptops, watching the static camera screens as Teresa and Melissa ventured back out into the house.

The activity seemed to have died down; there was nothing to record in the dining room except a couple of mice scurrying behind a huge old china hutch as they entered, nothing in the old office but the smell of musty books.

They tried the parlor again, but the cold spot was still gone and nothing else seemed to be happening.

Out of the stillness sounded the loud creak of old wood. Teresa and Melissa looked at each other, cocking their heads toward the front hall.

Stairs? Melissa mouthed the word.

Teresa nodded, and they crept toward the old staircase leading up into the pitch-black darkness of the second floor.

A minute passed, and then, further up the stairs, another ominous creak.

And then silence.

The girls waited, cameras pointed upward, Melissa using hers to scan back and forth, up the stairs and back again, but nothing moved. No sounds broke the silence.

After a few minutes, they sighed and headed back toward the kitchen.

"Hey," Teresa called over her shoulder. "Check the thermostat again, just in case."

Melissa stopped, pulling out her flashlight and aimed it at the dial.

"Whoa. Teresa, come look."

Teresa backtracked and peered at the numbers. She pulled out her notebook and checked the note she'd made earlier. Her eyes met Melissa's; eyebrows raised.

She made another note below the first, then rushed to the kitchen to show the others.

"See?" she said, holding the small notebook in the light so Jackson and Carrie could see it.

"That's a nine-degree change from what it was set on before!"

Jackson was skeptical. "Could be it's just programmed to different temperatures for different times of the day."

Teresa rolled her eyes. "That thing has to be fifty years old, man. I don't think they made programmable ones that long ago."

Jackson thought for a moment. "Well, that could be the problem right there. If it's fifty years old, maybe it's just dying. Maybe the dial like… is loose or something, spins slowly on its own over time."

"I guess maybe that could be it," Teresa admitted.

"Guys, I really don't feel so good." Carrie spoke softly. "Are we almost done here? I really just kind of want to go home and lay down."

"How about we try one more EVP session, and then if nothing comes up, we'll take you home?"

Melissa looked at Carrie with concern. The younger girl looked like she might fall over at any minute. Carrie nodded.

Teresa and Melissa sat in the middle of the hallway, just beyond the yellow light from the kitchen. They took turns asking questions, waiting for responses. They returned to the kitchen, listened back through the headphones.

Nothing.

"OK, let's pack it up, I guess. It's not even midnight but… yeah, let's get Carrie home." Teresa was disappointed, but she thought of the cold spot and the stairs creaking clear and loud into the quiet of the house.

We're coming back, though, she thought, that old lady swore there was weird stuff happening in her house, and we're going to get to the bottom of it.

As they locked up and loaded their equipment into the van, Teresa looked up at the house, a hulking shape, black against the night sky, silent and cold.

Oh, yes, make no mistake.

We'll be back, she told the old house, silently.

CHAPTER ONE

Millie

On a dark night, in an old house, at the top of a tall hill, Millie Carver woke with a start.

She didn't sleep much these days, but she didn't seem to be awake much, either. For her, the days and nights passed in one long, unending solitude; light and dark merging together. Her entire world took on a sort of twilit glow, till time itself seemed to slow and stretch and her mind wandered.

She had been born in that house, in 1929, the second in what would become a family of five children. She had grown up there, married, moved away, and eventually, as if the house exerted a magnetic pull upon her life that she could not escape, she had come back.

Not counting the few years she'd spent in a tiny bungalow in town starting her own small family, Millie had lived in the house at the end of the road for something like eighty years.

Eight decades of memories were contained within those walls. Sometimes the memories seemed to run from her, slipping half-glimpsed along the long hallways and through half-open doors, down the dark back stairwell or up into the dusty attic, pieces of herself she couldn't quite grab hold of.

Other times, times like tonight, her mind was clearer, alert, and the days of her life were there in sharp relief, ready to be picked up, caressed, lovingly remembered or cast hurriedly aside.

Everything in this house held a memory. Every creaking step, every dusty picture frame, every chipped dish in the kitchen cabinet.

And these days, memories were the only companions Millie had.

She had managed to outlive all her friends, not that she'd had many to begin with. She was what in her day they had called *shy*, what today the young people called *introverted*.

She'd had her house and her husband and her children, her books and her garden, and as far as she was concerned, that was all she'd ever really needed.

Other people just distracted her from those things.

Oh, they'd had a social life of sorts. Her husband, Arthur, God rest his soul, had been a little friendlier than she, and had dragged her on numerous occasions to various events in town.

And of course, they'd always gone to church together, at the little Baptist church on Hill Street in town.

When Millie reached the age of fifty-two, her son Mitch had moved out, off to college – and parties and dating. After college was med school; a doctor in the family.

Millie had been so proud until she found out just exactly what kind of doctor her son had become. A psychiatrist, one of those *head doctors*, who do people more harm than good and dope them up on handfuls of pills that make them walk around like zombies.

No, thank you.

Things with Mitch were always a little strained once he became Dr. Mitch Carver, MD.

When Millie was fifty-nine, and Mitch was away learning how to shrink people's heads, her daughter Suzanne moved out.

Two years at the local junior college and then she was off on the road with some leftover hippies who hadn't realized that the long-haired, peace-loving days were already over.

Two years after that, when Mitch was halfway through his residency, Suzanne came slinking back to town, thin and tired, and settled down into a life of relative respectability by marrying a real estate agent and doing all his clerical work in the office that was attached to their modest home.

By the time Millie turned sixty, she had resigned herself to the fact that she would never be a grandmother. Mitch just didn't have the time to worry about family, and Suzanne had finally told her that she couldn't have children.

Suzanne's head had hung low when she revealed this news, and her eyes had shifted around the room, avoiding her mother's gaze.

Millie had always secretly suspected that Suzanne had done something bad while she was off traipsing around California with those tree huggers. Something that had messed her up good inside, scrambled her lady parts and ended any chance she had of producing a child.

But of course Millie kept these thoughts to herself.

When Millie turned sixty-four, she became a widow.

There was no great story to tell, simply that Arthur was nearing seventy and his body had enough, succumbed, and gave up the ghost one cold January day.

The snow had been falling so thick and so long that the old road out to the house was impassable for three days.

Millie sat alone in the house with Arthur's body till the van from the funeral home could come gliding in on tires newly wrapped in chains.

Her children thought that she had never been quite the same since then.

Perhaps they were right.

CHAPTER TWO

Millie

It was snowing again.

Millie was bundled against the cold, in thick socks and a flannel nightgown, with a quilted dressing gown over that, and a shawl over that.

The old house needed work; it was drafty. Perhaps she could get Mitch to come and do some things, fix it up a bit, but no, of course not. His doctor's hands weren't used to hard labor.

Neither, for that matter, were the hands of Suzanne's husband, Gerry.

The hardest work he'd ever done was hammering a 'For Sale' sign into a yard.

Millie shook her head. *Men these days.*

There were some things she could fix herself, though. She was no weak woman, even at the age of eighty…oh, eighty-something.

She might not be able to hammer boards anymore, but even she could manage to caulk around some drafty windows.

She was sure there was a box of caulking tubes down in the basement, left over from the days when Arthur was still around to fix things for her. Would it still be good? Did caulk go bad?

She didn't know.

Millie lifted herself slowly from the armchair she'd woken up in. Though it hurt to move, her body felt light. She hadn't been eating much lately. Not on purpose, she wasn't one of those old women who did things just to get attention and sympathy.

No, she simply didn't have much appetite.

A cup of warm tea and some toast seemed to be her favorite meal these days.

Her slippers made pleasant shooshing sounds against the carpet as she walked. In the whole house, only this one room, the parlor, was carpeted.

Millie quick-stepped a few times, feeling the soft springiness of the fibers beneath her feet, one side of her mouth turning up in the memory of a smile.

In her mind, she was eleven years old again, watching excitedly as the contractors worked in the emptied parlor, her mother's fine furniture stacked neatly against the walls of the adjoining hallway.

There were the loud ringing of hammers and the low, gruff voices of the men as they worked.

Out the open front door she could see the huge roll of red carpeting waiting to be installed. Cranberry red, her mother had called it. *Blood red*, her brother Davey had said.

Mother had given him *the look* and informed him that they would have no such talk in their house. But Davey was right, Millie had thought – silently, to herself, of course – it was the color of blood.

It had taken the men the better part of a day to get the carpet work done, and then Mother had made all the children stand back out of the way while Father moved all the furniture back in before she would let them enter the room and walk on it.

It scared little Laura, who was only three. She refused to enter the parlor. She cried and pointed and said, in her little child's voice, "Bloody floor! Bloody floor!"

Then she'd hidden her face in Mother's skirts while Mother gave Davey another *look* that said she'd be having a serious talk with him very soon.

That night, Millie had slipped quietly from her bed, crept down the stairs, careful to avoid the third and the tenth, as you came down (which was of course different numbers - the sixth and the thirteenth - as you went up,

Millie had learned the hard way) which everyone knew
were the loud, creaky stairs that must be avoided during
secret late-night shenanigans.

She had stopped at the threshold of the parlor, the
blood-red carpet nearly black in the darkness and had
taken off her slippers.

Holding her breath, she stepped gingerly, first one bare
foot and then the other, into the heavenly softness of the
carpet.

She had walked circles around the edge of the room for
ten minutes, her feet sinking into the luxurious pile,
feeling like a queen in a castle, feeling like the ruler of the
world.

Then she had slid her feet back into her slippers and
crept quietly back up the stairs to bed. Her mother would
have had a fit if she had known that Millie was walking
about barefooted.

It wasn't ladylike.

The next day, Mother had proclaimed the parlor off
limits except when company came. With the fear of a
sound spanking looming large in their minds, the children
obeyed.

The parlor sat empty and unused until visitors came.

Except, of course, for the many times Millie had crept
down the stairs to steal a few moments of barefoot
happiness.

A quiet chuckle escaped her mouth now as she thought about it. She wasn't taking her slippers off now to walk barefoot through the carpet though, it was too damn cold.

Yes, she reminded herself, *the caulk in the basement.*

As she made her way slowly down the front hallway, a sudden feeling of unease made her stop, a hand against the wall to steady herself, ears straining.

Had she heard something in the kitchen? She stood motionless in the quiet, her old eyes narrowed and peering into the yellow glow of the kitchen.

Had she left the light on in there? Its dim yellow glow radiated out into the hall, so she must have.

Seemed unlike her, though, to waste electricity like that.

Her father always said, "Until you learn to harness the lightning, Millie, the house lights don't come free."

Shaking her head at her own negligence, Millie made her way further down the long hall.

To her right, the old round Honeywell thermostat glinted with reflected light. Millie stopped and peered at it. Sixty-five degrees! In November!

Why, it was probably down around freezing outdoors. No wonder it was so blasted cold in her house. How did that happen?

Her eyes narrowed.

Had Suzanne or her silly husband been here? Surely not Mitch? But no one else had keys to her house.

Unless…

Suddenly Millie felt frightened, an old woman all alone in a house a good two miles distant from the town.

Had someone been here, in her house? In *her* house? Was someone *still* here?

Her eyes shot to the light shining in the kitchen. Her breath hitched in her throat; her knees felt weak even as a rush of adrenaline coursed its way through her old veins.

Cautiously she approached the kitchen.

Nothing looked out of place. The back door was locked firmly against the black night.

Millie breathed quietly as her old lungs would allow, turning slowly on the spot to take in the whole room until her eyes fell on the basement door.

Could someone be down there?

She sidled up close to the door, listening.

The locks were securely in place. She had always made sure it was locked when her children were little, out of an abundance of caution, as the basement stairs were old and steep, and the handrail only went halfway down before opening up into the space below.

She'd had nightmares about little Mitch falling down those stairs and cracking his head open, once he began to toddle about the house, so at her insistence, Arthur had installed two heavy sliding locks, high up beyond the reach of small children, to ease her fears.

Both locks were slid completely shut.

And yet.

Millie could not shake the feeling that something was wrong.

Silly old bat, she chided herself. She was just an old woman, growing forgetful and jumping at shadows.

Giving the locks one last glance, she made her way slowly back down the hall.

At the thermostat she stopped, arthritic hand reaching up to turn the dial to the left, setting the temperature to 74 degrees. How *had* it gotten turned down to sixty-six?

Maybe the old thermostat was dying. She'd have to get someone out to fix it. But that could wait till tomorrow.

For now, she decided, all her aching bones needed was to force themselves up the stairs (the sixth and the thirteenth creaking as she made her way) and to burrow under the nice warm blankets on her bed.

At the second-floor landing, she paused and looked down over the railing.

Blast it!

A glow from the kitchen still reached, pale and yellow, to the front of the house.

Oh, well. Nothing for it now.

She didn't dare try the stairs again. Already she could feel her body giving out, her mind slipping into sleep.

Best just hurry to bed.

Troubles could wait till tomorrow.

CHAPTER THREE

Millie

The windows were covered in frost.

Sneaking through a crack in the drapes, the pale glow of a chill November morning filtered through the ice crystals and made a stripe of light along Millie's bedroom wall.

She lay on the bed, curled onto her side, still wearing her flannel gown, her quilted dressing gown, her old shawl, and three thick quilts besides, bundled around her against the cold.

Her eyes were on the strip of light. It seemed to her that she had slept for days, or perhaps only for minutes. In her mind time shrank and expanded.

Yesterday seemed like years ago and things that she knew happened decades past spring to mind with the freshness of last week.

The strip of light cut a perfectly centered line down an old photograph that hung on the wall.

On one side of the light, her mother, young and smiling. On the other side, her father, young and serious. Had her father ever smiled? She couldn't really remember.

Oh, surely he had, but it would have been rare. And the truth was, her mother didn't smile much either.

Her mother smiled in this photo, of course, but that was when she had been young and carefree, a new wife with a new house and no children to drain her energy and muddy up her kitchen floors and cause her no end of aggravation.

Millie chuckled to herself, lying under the quilts. That was what her mother always said: "These children cause me no end of aggravation."

Millie supposed they had, indeed.

But as a grown woman herself, Millie had come to see that the real thing that aggravated her mother was her father.

Martin Carver had come from money – his grandfather had owned one of the largest farms in Macon County, his fields in the fertile land around Macon Lake, and he had grown the farm into a business, selling crops and renting out equipment, buying up more land and leasing it to smaller farmers.

By the time Martin had been born, just after the nineteenth century rolled over to the twentieth, the Carvers were the richest family for a hundred miles, living in the huge house on the hill, though the farmland itself had shrunk.

When Millie's mother, Helen, first met Martin, she didn't know he came from all that money. She didn't know he lived in the biggest house around, or that he could have any girl in town he wanted because of it.

All she knew was that her family had just moved to town, and he was the first young man to speak to her, and be kind to her, and smile his irresistible smile at her.

Millie had heard the story so many times growing up that she knew it by heart. Her parents – not parents then, barely even adults, how young and beautiful and happy they had been.

She'd heard the story of how her father had swept her mother off her feet. How he'd shocked his family and friends by asking her to marry him just two months after they met.

She had heard the stories of the wedding on the lawn out back, under the giant pecan trees. How he'd taken her all the way to St. Louis in his Model T, stopping along the way for a picnic lunch on the side of the road; how he had laughed when the thing she most wanted to do in the city was to visit the giant Central Library, and told her that he would gladly buy her any books she wanted.

She was a Carver now and didn't have to borrow books from other people.

Yes, Martin Carver had come from money, and when he married the beautiful Helen Gorse, in 1922, he'd had plenty.

When their firstborn, Davey, was born in 1924, he'd had even more.

When Millie herself had been born, in 1929, he'd had a few hard months, but still had plenty.

By the time their third child was born in 1932, he'd had less.

And then less.

And then less.

The stock market crash hadn't affected them like it had many others. The effects of the Great Depression were not so sudden and severe, but there were effects just the same.

Martin's father had taken some of the money from the farm and invested it. The crash did away with that. Their financial future was suddenly less secure.

The people who bought their produce had less money to spend. The small farmers who rented land from the family couldn't pay their rent.

Things had gotten tight in the Carver household.

Millie's father began to change. Born into wealth, raised in wealth, Martin hadn't known what to do when he found himself suddenly needing to pay attention to how much money he spent.

He had become depressed, and then he had become angry.

And then he had taken his anger out on his wife.

He never hit her, never did anything that would leave a mark, at least not where anyone could see.

No, what Martin Carver did to his wife was to blame her for everything.

If the kids cried, it was her fault for not attending to them fast enough. If dinner was late, it was her fault for being lazy.

If there was just enough money to pay the bills and none left over for pleasure, it was her fault for not managing their accounts better.

Helen Martin had simply smiled and apologized and promised to be better. For forty years she had made those promises.

Millie opened her eyes.

The stripe of light had made its way down the wall, along the floor, where it now sat tight against the opposite wall, just under the window.

The day was passing. She thought about getting up, going downstairs, fixing a cup of nice warm tea.

The quilts made a comforting weight against her.

Millie closed her eyes.

CHAPTER FOUR

Millie

Millie sat on the side of the bed, scrunching her toes inside her fuzzy slippers.

She didn't know how long she'd been asleep. There was a clear glow coming through the gap in the drapes, but it looked like moonlight. Had she slept through the entire day?

She shook her head at her increasing inability to keep track of time.

Pushing off the bed, she shuffled to the window and peeked out. Yes, moonlight. A half circle glowing in the sky.

She leaned against the glass, gazing upward. The sky was blue – midnight blue, they called it – and it only looked that particular color in the cold part of the year.

During the summer the sky was simply black at night. Millie didn't care much for summer. Too hot. Too many mosquitoes.

But as soon as the air began to cool and the leaves began to turn, and the sunlight slanted in sideways and made the shadows grow long, as soon as autumn arrived, Millie was always happy.

She felt happy now, she realized. A hundred wrinkles creased her face as she smiled.

Autumn was always the best time when she was younger.

As a child it meant that school started, and Millie was one of those rare children who loved school: the smell of chalk dust and pencil shavings, old books and new ones, reading and learning things.

When she was older and attending high school, there were committees and dances and trips to the movies with her friends when there was a tiny bit of extra money to go round.

Oh, they'd rolled up their stockings and brushed out their pin curls and made themselves up as best they could and strolled down Main Street arm in arm to the Carousel Theater.

They'd cried over Jane Eyre, shrieked during Cry of the Werewolf, and when they watched Tall in the Saddle, Millie had secretly fawned over the handsome young John Wayne.

And of course, autumn was the time she'd met Arthur.

His family had moved to town in the summer of 1946, just before school started.

Arthur was a quiet young man, not loud and always messing about in the halls like most of the other boys, and it didn't take long at all for every girl in the school to start gossiping about the mysterious new student.

They'd spoken for the first time in the library; quiet whispers over books.

One day at the end of September, he'd worked up the courage to ask her if she wanted to stop for a soda after school, and that was that.

They'd been inseparable from them on.

Millie knew the other girls were all jealous, and she hadn't cared.

Two years later, on a perfect October day, they were married in the Baptist church.

Millie shuffled her way over to the Victrola in the corner of her bedroom. The old 45 vinyl was already on the turntable.

She gently lifted the needle and placed it at the edge of the record.

A burst of static, then Nat King Cole's voice began crooning "I Love You for Sentimental Reasons."

She and Arthur had danced to it on the night he proposed, and again almost a year later at their wedding.

Humming and swaying in time to the music – back and forth, back and forth – Millie closed her eyes and lost herself in reverie.

She could feel the solid warmth of Arthur's body against hers, his arms around her, could hear him laugh as her hair tickled his cheek, could feel the rush as he tilted her chin up and kissed her full on the mouth to the applause of everyone around them.

"Now then, Mrs. Carver, what do you say we get out of this place and away from all these people?"

She smiled at the memory, at the sudden flush that had flooded her cheeks, the excitement, the nervousness as they'd left their families and friends standing on the street outside the church and driven off together, headed for their honeymoon in Springfield.

Millie's father had grudgingly handed over the money for a weekend stay.

Millie's eyes flew open as the needle scratched its way to the edge of the record and the music stopped.

Silly old woman, she chided herself, *living in memories.* But they were good memories, weren't they?

She'd had a good life. Married a good man. Kept a nice house, raised two good kids.

They were good kids, weren't they? Even if they rarely came around anymore.

Well, Mitch was busy with his doctoring and Suzanne had her husband to look after and a business to help run and… yes. They were still good kids.

She had done her best to raise them right. Not perfect, maybe, but still good.

With a shrug of her shoulders, Millie turned away from the Victrola. She pulled her shawl closer around her, shuffled out of the bedroom and made her way slowly, holding tightly to the banister with both hands, down the stairs.

Time for tea.

She stopped at the bottom of the stairs and listened. Hadn't something happened last time she was down here? What had it been? A sound? A movement?

In the back of her mind she had a vague recollection of being disturbed by something, but she couldn't quite remember what.

Everything seemed to be in order down here, and there were no strange sounds that she could hear at the moment, so she continued on toward the kitchen.

Millie shuffled to the stove and reached for the tea kettle.

Her hand hovered in midair, inches above the handle. Her heart sped up inside her chest.

She didn't quite know why, but she had the distinct feeling that someone was standing directly behind her.

Eyes darting left and right, mouth tight against her toothless gums, she dropped her hand and grasped the handle of the kettle tightly.

She swung around as quickly as she could, the arm with the kettle making a feeble arc through the air a moment behind the rest of her body.

There was no one there.

She clutched the kettle to her chest and reminded herself to breathe.

Something was definitely not right.

Though she couldn't see anyone or anything out of place, Millie *knew* that something was off. Her eyes slid to the basement door.

There was something about the basement door, wasn't there? Last time? Hadn't it frightened her, somehow?

Her mind was full of cobwebs, memories caught up and twisted together in tangles she could not unravel.

But there was definitely something about the basement door.

She inched her way toward it, kettle still in hand. She checked that both locks were slid securely into place. She grasped the doorknob and rattled it, making the door creak against the locks, but it held firmly.

Still she could not shake the feeling that someone was down there.

But no one could be down there. How could they be? The outer entrance to the basement, the one that used to open into the backyard, had been sealed up and bricked over decades ago.

The only other way in was through this door, and it was locked from this side.

Millie's mind flooded suddenly with images from old movies she'd seen, hazy ethereal figures floating through walls and doors like the barriers weren't there.

Come now, really? Ghosts?

She gave a derisive snort, but inside her chest her heart still pounded, and her legs were beginning to feel wobbly.

A rush of cold air settled over her. She leaned against the door, pressing her fingertips against it's solid wood, and held her ear up close.

She listened.

Could she hear anything? Of course not. Except… with the whole weight of her body pressed against the door, her ear scratched by the grain of the wood, she thought that perhaps she *could* hear something.

Was that… a voice?

Goosebumps prickled her body. She covered her other ear with her hand to block out any noise but the voice – if it was a voice.

Yes! Faintly, a voice. A woman's voice. Was there a woman *in her basement*?

And if there was, who was she talking to? Was there more than one person down there? She needed to call the police, and she needed to do it right now.

But as Millie straightened and stepped away from the door, the voices got louder. She froze in place, fear flooding her veins like acid.

The voices were definitely louder from out in the kitchen. They weren't in the basement at all.

The voices were a jumble, cadence-like words but no words that Millie could understand.

It wasn't a foreign language, it was more like… well, she realized, like listening to Charlie Brown's teacher speak in those old cartoons.

Wah, wah-wah, wah wah.

Millie had to force the breaths in and out through her nose. She didn't dare move, didn't dare draw attention to herself and didn't dare try to flee because she felt sure her legs would simply fold underneath her and she'd fall.

She eyed the telephone on the opposite wall of the kitchen, next to the back door. She would have to make it that far, at least.

The voices – if she could trust her ears at all, which she certainly wasn't sure about – were just beyond the kitchen. In the hallway? The parlor? Maybe they were outside!

Yes! Her mind latched on to this thought.

Probably teenagers messing about outside. Indignance shot through her fear. What were they doing on her property?

What were they *planning* to do?

Invigorated by anger, she hobbled around the edge of the kitchen, one hand on the counters to help steady her as she went.

She grabbed the old green phone receiver from its cradle and put it to her ear.

Silence. There was no dial tone.

Had those hooligans cut her phone line? But the silence was not only on the line… Millie paused, waited, listened.

Silence everywhere. The voices had stopped. Had they seen her in the kitchen? Were they outside right now, just beyond the windows, watching her every move? What could she do? How could she –

A loud knocking sound made her jump. Like someone knocking at a door but not quite like that.

The sound seemed to come from everywhere. From the walls, from the floor, from the old wooden table where she used to sit and chop vegetables for dinner.

Moments passed. The grandfather clock in the hall ticked loudly in the silence.

Again it came: *knock, knock.*

Silence.

Knock, knock.

Millie's head was spinning, her heart pumping blood through her body faster than it had in twenty years, her breath coming in short shaking bursts.

She didn't know what was happening, her mind struggling for an answer, a reason, an explanation, but all it could seem to settle on was the one idea it simultaneously rejected: *her house was haunted.*

Knock, knock.

Her house was *haunted.*

Knock, knock.

Her *house* was haunted.

Knock, knock.

Her house was haunted.

"It's *my* house!" she yelled suddenly, the words slipping out before she knew she was going to say them.

"It's my damn house!"

She rapped her own knuckles once, twice, against the wall – knock, knock!

"It's my house! Mine! Leave me alone!"

She did it again – knock, knock! – against the glass window of the back door.

Silence.

Millie jumped as the grandfather clock sounded.

She slumped to the floor; her energy gone.

Blackness crowded the edges of her vision. Her hand twitched and the kettle rolled slowly across her lap and clanged against the floor. Her eyes closed.

CHAPTER FIVE
Millie

There was sunlight coming through the crack in the drapes again.

Millie groaned beneath the quilts. One eye cracked open, then the other. Her body was numb, still asleep though her mind was waking up.

The light crept in from the front window this time, a stripe that ran up the lumpy shape that was her body beneath the blankets and suffused the back of her eyelids with a tangerine glow.

Millie turned her head away from the brightness.

She struggled to come up out of the deep pit of slumber. Her mind dipped in and out of consciousness as the sun outside her window sunk lower and lower, the strip of light turning from orange to red to purple before disappearing completely.

In the darkness her eyes snapped open again. Something. Something in her house. A wave of prickling cold ran down her skin. There had been something, hadn't there? Someone? No, something.

Her breath hitched in her throat as the memory came back in disjointed flashes. There had been voices. And an awful knocking sound. She had been so afraid, and so angry.

She… she had yelled at it, hadn't she? Yelled at whatever it was that was scaring her. Told it to go away. And it had.

Hadn't it?

Millie pushed herself upright and swung her bottom half slowly over the side of the bed. Her spindly legs stuck out beneath her nightgown, pale skin shining in the darkness. She twisted her back first one way, then the other, stretching the tight muscles. It seemed cold in the house again.

Her bones felt frozen right down to the marrow.

Bracing herself against the mattress, she stood up. For a brief moment the darkened room seemed to swim around her, swirling left then right before settling.

God, she was old.

Slowly and carefully, Millie shuffled across the room and out into the hallway. She listened closely but heard only the familiar creaks and groans of the old house settling.

She ran her hand along the wallpaper and gave it a kindly pat.

"You're even older than me, old house. We both creak a little these days."

The house seemed to sigh and settle in response to her words, and a long-forgotten memory passed through her mind.

She and Davey, only small children, creeping along the hallways and searching out the best places to hide in the huge old house.

Hide-and-seek had been their favorite game for a while, although Dave, with the advantage of being five years older, was always better. He moved faster and thought smarter, and he certainly could stay quietly hidden much longer than she ever could.

She'd break into a fit of giggles the moment he came anywhere near her hiding spot.

A distinctly girlish giggle escaped her now, though it ended in a sound which seemed more like a sob. *Oh, Davey. Poor Davey.*

Millie turned away from the stairs and padded down to the bedroom that used to be his. It hadn't changed since the day he'd left it.

Her parents had been too grieved to do anything else with it, and when she and Arthur had moved in and taken the house as their own, her own heart was too broken by the thought of erasing his presence from the house to change it, either.

With five bedrooms and only two children, they hadn't needed the room anyway, so she'd had Arthur fit it with one of those small hook and eye locks, high up, so the children couldn't intrude, and that was that.

She had gone into the room now and then as time passed, dusting and sweeping and fluffing the blankets on the bed, but it had been years now since she'd done that.

Decades, maybe.

The old hook was rusty in its metal eye, and she had to work it back and forth a few times before it would release. The door swung open with a slight creak.

The cold seemed deeper inside, and the musty smell of dust and old linens worked its way into Millie's nostrils. She scrunched up her nose and felt along the wall for the light switch.

The ancient bulb buzzed and slowly came to life, flickering a few times before settling into a dull glow. Millie took in a deep breath, let it out slowly.

Davey, such a sweet boy. Such a fun and rambunctious child. In his younger days he had been king of the hill, the leader of the gang of boys he ran about town with, the one always with the best ideas of places to go and games to play.

Millie had looked up to him adoringly, and he had been a good big brother. He had always made a little time to play with her each day, hide-and-seek in the dark hallways or pirate adventures in the backyard; he had even, once or twice, deigned to play house with her, dutifully rocking the baby dolls she brought to him.

And then things had changed.

Davey was fifteen when Germany attacked Poland and set off that awful chain of events that would become the Second World War.

He was seventeen when the Japs bombed Pearl Harbor, forcing the States into the fray. He was eighteen when he left.

He was twenty when his troop was ordered to the fight that would become known as the Battle of the Bulge. And he was twenty when he died.

Millie walked across the dusty floor to Davey's old desk. She picked up the triangular wooden frame that held his burial flag. Using the sleeve of her dressing gown, she wiped dust from the top and the glass front. Beneath the dull glass, the flag still showed its vibrant colors.

A pain shot through Millie's heart and her eyes burned with the tears that formed there; her voice was barely more than a whisper: "Oh, Davey."

She'd been fifteen when he died, old enough to understand but still young enough to hope against hope that they were wrong and he would come back, that one day the doorbell would ring and there he would stand, tall and strong in his uniform, smiling and opening his arms as she rushed to hug him.

Of course that was a foolish, childish dream. She'd known it, deep down, at fifteen, and she knew even more, knew it with an agonizing ache, now that she was an old woman.

In her mind a song began to play.

I'll be seeing you... in all the old familiar places... that this heart of mine embraces...

A memory: Billie Holiday's smooth voice on the Victrola, Davey home on leave the summer of 1944, young and handsome, dancing with his sister, laughing and alive, telling her not to worry, he'd be fine, he'd be careful, he'd be safe, he'd be home again before she knew it, and he'd be seeing her in all those old familiar places.

She had smiled at him then, the war still yet a far-off thing that only touched her briefly, distantly.

In the light of the dim bulb, Millie pressed the flag case against her chest and hummed along to the tune while hot tears ran down her face:

I'll be seeing you... in every lovely summer's day... in everything that's light and gay... I'll always think of you that way...

When the song in her head had faded and the tears on her cheeks had dried, Millie set the flag case carefully down in its spot on the desk.

She gazed around the room, her eyes lingering lovingly, sadly, on the neatly made bed, the shelf of trophies, the stack of comic books tucked away under the bedside table.

A whole life, a short life, contained in this one room.

It occurred to her that her life was much the same: a longer life, certainly, and spread out over more rooms than one, but all of it contained within this old house.

She'd follow Davey one of these days, leave behind rooms full of her things, her memories, her essence. Some days she longed for death.

Life didn't seem like much to hang on to anymore, just one long endless cycle of sleeping and waking, eating and drinking, remembering and forgetting.

Slowly, she pulled the door to Davey's bedroom closed behind her and fitted the hook into its eye with a shaking hand.

She rubbed her hands across her face a few times, wiping away errant tears; memories and love and loss contained in salt water.

Yes, she'd follow him in death someday. But not today.

Today she was still alive, still standing.

Millie made her way down the creaky old stairs. She glanced into each room along the downstairs hall as she passed; the parlor, the office, the dining room: all seemed in order.

She stopped to peer again at the thermostat and clucked her tongue in disapproval. It had been changed. Again.

Must be getting old and worn out and not working quite right anymore.

Just like her.

She spun the dial a few degrees and continued down the hall.

The light was on again in the kitchen. This puzzled her for a brief moment, but she seemed to remember it being on the last time she was here, and she didn't remember turning it off, so the puzzle, she decided, was simply her own old brain.

It was strange how she could remember things that happened fifty or sixty years ago with such clarity, but she couldn't remember what she did yesterday except in vague scattered pieces of time.

In the kitchen she made herself a cup of tea, going through the motions by rote, filling the kettle and setting it to boil, dropping a tiny tea bag into an old porcelain cup, pouring in the hot water and waiting while the tea steeped.

She loved the smell of tea leaves.

When Mitch and Suzanne were small children, she would open up the box of Lipton and take three bags out, giving them each one to press against their noses and sniff. They'd inhale the strong, sweet fragrance and sigh, then the children would hand back their tea bags and run off to play while she made the tea.

Such lovely times. Life was made up of such sadness and such lovely times, mixed together.

Millie sighed.

She knew from the darkness that it was late in the night, but it seemed she'd slept all day again, so she thought she might go sit in the parlor for a bit and read a book.

She kept her favorites stacked on the fireplace mantel where she could easily find them. The books were dustier than she'd like, and she scolded herself for letting the house get so dirty.

But she was only one old woman, after all, in a huge house. Maybe she could convince Suzanne to come up and help her clean one day soon.

She made up her mind to call her daughter in the morning, at a decent hour when decent people were awake. The thought made her chuckle. Apparently she was not a decent person, often being awake at all kinds of indecent hours.

Her fingers ran along the spines of the books and chose one at random. She could just make out the gilt writing on the front: *Anne of Green Gables*. Ah, one of her favorites since childhood.

She could lose herself in that story for an hour or two.

But what was that?

Her hand hovered halfway on its course to pull the chain on the old lamp next to her favorite chair. She could swear she'd heard a noise.

Something moving out in the hall.

She dropped her book onto the chair and approached the hall doorway cautiously.

Very faintly she could hear something. Voices, perhaps, murmuring; or something like an appliance humming and knocking?

It was quiet and distant, like listening through an old phone line, the sound tinny and distorted. She crept down the hall, sliding along the wall.

The sound seemed to grow louder as she neared the kitchen.

Was it mice? Mice knocking about in the cabinets, chewing through boxes and eating all her good food?

She had traps somewhere, she knew, down in the basement probably. Arthur would have had some there, yes.

And then the noise was gone.

No murmuring, no scurrying movement, no knocking about. The mice must have heard her and hidden away in their hidey-holes.

In her walls!

To think that mice were living in her walls, leaving their nasty little droppings all over her house.

She shuddered. Well, when she called Suzanne tomorrow to ask for help cleaning, she'd mention the mice, too.

That might help spur Suzanne to hurry up and come.

With all quiet at the back end of the house, Millie trudged back to the parlor. All this back and forth was making her tired.

Her aching joints just wanted to sit for a bit, sit and not move. Come to think of it, she was getting sleepy again, too. She might just lay her head back and have a bit of a cat nap in the armchair.

Settled in, her gowns and shawls arranged around her and her feet nestled in her warm slippers, she rested her head against the tall sides of the chair and closed her eyes.

Outside, the wind was blowing; a thousand dead leaves scraping over each other as they shuffled around the edges of the house.

Another thing she needed help with, of course.

Maybe she'd tell Suzanne to bring her husband along as well. He could do the outdoor work while she and Suzanne cleaned. She had never really liked having him inside the house.

His realtor's eyes ran greedily over the tall ceilings and the hardwood floors and the original stained glass transom windows.

She could practically see him rubbing his hands and licking his lips over the crown moldings and the carved newel posts and the built-in bookshelves.

Yes, she knew that he couldn't wait to get his hands on this house, knew that he'd convince Suzanne to sell it the moment the deed was in her name.

No, she didn't like having him in the house at all.

Of course Mitch wasn't much better. He couldn't be bothered to come to his hometown, much less his own childhood home. He wouldn't want to live in the house when she died.

He wouldn't even want to leave his precious practice to come to her funeral!

Her eyebrows pulled down as her mind worked through these thoughts, her forehead creasing in countless tiny wrinkles.

She ought to just cut them both off – leave the house to the town as a historical site or something. She smiled at the thought. But of course she'd never really do that.

She'd leave it to Suzanne, as her will said, and what they did with it after she was gone was their business. She'd be past caring at that point, tripping along golden streets in heaven with Arthur at her side.

The thought made her happy; her body relaxed against the chair and her mind wandered to the edge of sleep.

She jerked so suddenly that she banged her elbow against the carved wooden arm of the chair. Her heart was beating fast.

The noise that woke her sounded again, close by.

Knock, knock!

Oh, Lord, not this again.

Her jaw quivered and she braced herself stiffly against the chair, hands curling around the armrests, eyes squeezed tightly shut as she waited for it to come again.

Knock, knock!

It was just kids, last time, wasn't it? Silly teenagers out pulling pranks, trying to scare an old woman? Wasn't it? Or was it?

Her mind searched around in the dark recesses of recent memory. Had it been something else? The thought, the memory, suddenly blazed forth and shouted inside her head: *my house is haunted!*

Knock.

The sound came from all around her, vibrating through the walls and shaking the windowpanes.

Knock, knock.

But why, why would her house be haunted? Who would possibly haunt it? Davey? Oh! The thought made her heart leap within her chest. Could it be? But why now?

She'd lived in this house for decades and never heard a ghostly peep before. Was it… Arthur?

Oh, God, it could be Mother or Father or any of her other siblings. Carol, Jack, Laura? But no, it didn't make sense!

Why would they, why would any of them come back to haunt her, to scare her, to torment her like this?

Knock!

Millie's hand stretched out and she rapped her knuckles against the wall, once, twice: knock, knock!
She waited.

A minute passed.

"Davey? Is that you? Is this another one of your games? Or Arthur, darling? It is you, come back to me?"

Another minute of silence. And then: *knock, knock!* Just inside the doorway.

Millie rapped again in response: knock, knock, knock!

She strained her ears. "Mother? Father? Oh, who is it? Who is here? What do you want?"

A few beats of silence, and then she heard it again: *knock!* Further inside the room this time, somewhere near the fireplace.

Millie's fist pounded the wall beside her chair, each bang accentuating her words as she cried out: *Who –* knock! – *are* - knock! – *you?* – knock! *What* – knock! – *do* - knock! – *you-* knock! – *want?* – knock! – *Why* – knock! – *are* – knock! *You* – knock! *here?* - knock! knock! knock!

But the house had gone silent around her, and Millie was left alone with her tears and frustrations.

CHAPTER SIX

Suzanne

Suzanne was busy as usual.

She stayed busy, really, to keep her mind off things, mostly the fact that her life was a complete and total disappointment.

When a potential customer walked through the door of their little real estate office, she plastered on a fake smile and coughed up a sickly-sweet professional voice.

She typed up Gerry's emails and filed away his paperwork. She tidied her desk and swept the floor of the office and dusted the plasticky potted plant that sat in the corner.

She pulled a bottle of Windex from beneath the small bathroom's sink and cleaned the front windows, and then defied any little urchin to come walking down Main Street and smear his dirty fingerprints on her freshly cleaned glass.

But whenever a child did come skipping down Main Street – a four-year-old tugging on his mother's hand, or a trio of rowdy ten-year-old boys, running and laughing on their way to the old-school arcade, or a happy little family, the father pushing a stroller with the mother looking on lovingly, the baby just a bundle of blankets with two eyes peeping our – Suzanne didn't hate them, not really.

She envied them.

She also envied the couples that came down the sidewalk together – young lovers who couldn't keep their hands off each other, or old couples, stooped and bent, walking slowly, he opening the door for her as they entered the diner across the street for the Early Bird Special.

That kind of love, that kind of joy, it wasn't for her. Oh, she'd have liked it to be for her, but it just wasn't the way her life had turned out.

No, her life had flung her first into the arms of Rocky – a handsome young man with big hair and wild dreams, then into the back of an old VW bus on the way to California, then into the grip of alcohol and drugs.

Then she had found herself on her back on an old exam table, with her legs up in the air, while a doctor with shifty eyes ripped apart her insides in the name of freedom.

After she'd gone home from the *procedure*, achy and sore and bleeding, Rocky had been angry.

He wasn't angry about the abortion, only that he'd had to pay so much for it.

And after a six pack, he was angry at her, angry at what he thought was her attempt to control him, to bind him to her through a child that neither of them really wanted.

When he was angry, he was violent.

And so finally life had dumped her, thin and trembling, at the bus station back here in Hillview, Missouri; her hair longer, her innocence gone, her head bowed, her eye blacked, and her womb never again to feel life quickening inside it.

Her mother had taken her back in, of course; she had to. If she hadn't, what would the people in town think?

Suzanne had hated living back in the big house with her mother just as much as her mother had hated having her there.

Or, if she was being fair, perhaps it wasn't hatred on either side, really, but disappointment maybe, and sadness, and an inability to properly communicate.

Whatever it was called, the few weeks she had spent back in the old house were miserable ones.

When she'd finally healed enough to be presentable in public, she'd been shopping for a few essentials at the small grocery store in town, staring listlessly at rows of stacked lettuces, when someone said her name.

She'd turned to find a young man, about her age, standing behind her, smiling. She hadn't recognized him at first, hadn't remembered the quiet boy she'd gone to school with just a few years before, hadn't known that for all four years of high school he'd been madly, secretly in love with her while she barely registered his existence.

But then, standing in that grocery store, finally recalling the barely-there memory of Gerry Bowles, a thought had occurred to her.

Gerry could be her ticket out of her mother's house. He was a nice enough guy, really. Not a supermodel, not handsome like Rocky had been, but attractive in an everyday sort of way.

After talking for a few minutes, she learned that at twenty-one years old, he was already a certified realtor and would be setting up shop here in town.

There was only one other real estate agency in the area, and that was run by an older couple who would be retiring any time now. Business should be good.

Nothing big, but steady work.

Yes, she'd decided, he could definitely be a decent guy to attach herself to. So she'd smiled her brightest smile and laughed at his jokes. She'd let him take her to dinner. She'd let him hold her hand, and eventually put his hand on her leg.

She'd learned not to flinch when his fingers touched her face, learned that he was as gentle and steadfast as Rocky had been wild and volatile.

And when he'd kneeled in front of her with a diamond ring in a velvet box, she'd smiled and said yes.

She had never hated him. But she didn't know if she had ever really loved him, either.

She'd had to tell him, of course, before they got married, that she would never be able to give him children.

He hadn't minded, he'd said; they would be perfectly happy together, just the two of them, and if they ever got to really wanting a child, they could always adopt.

But they hadn't.

They hadn't been perfectly happy together and they hadn't adopted.

They'd lived out their lives in the routine of the settled. Breakfasts, lunches, and dinners. Weekdays and weekends. Work and home. Winter into spring into summer into fall.

She'd kept the house and kept the books and done her best to keep him happy. She'd smiled at all the right times and said the right things, hosted the small dinner parties and weeded the sad little flower bed out front, made the right noises at the right times when they were alone in bed together at night.

He couldn't fault her, really.

She couldn't fault him, either. He had done his best.

He had loved her and tried to make her happy. And sometimes she was happy, but never really happy enough.

She thought now of her parents, of how happy *they* had seemed, dancing together in the kitchen at night, laughing and smiling and holding hands until the day her father died.

And she thought of her mother, of all the years spent alone in that house on the hill.

Suzanne thought of how she'd never visited her mother enough, not in all these years she'd been back in town, and she thought of how her mother hadn't really seemed to mind.

She'd thought about her a few days ago on Thanksgiving, thought about her and cried, thought about the fight they'd had at the last Thanksgiving, when the food had all been bland and half raw, and Suzanne had suggested that they try to have holidays at her house from now on.

Her mother wouldn't hear of it. She'd told them to get out and that they could celebrate holidays at their own house from now on if they wanted, but *she* would not be there.

That's what they had been doing, last Thursday, celebrating at home with a few friends, a modern potluck affair.

And while everyone else had been laughing and eating and clinking wine glasses, she'd been locked in the bathroom, thinking about her mother.

She thought now of how her mother always said that life was what you made it. She thought of how her mother had lived out that belief, and how she had managed to wrangle together a happy life for herself.

Then she thought of how she herself had failed at this, and it occurred to her, as the sun sank below the horizon and she locked the front door and flipped the sign from OPEN to CLOSED, that therein lay the real problem with her relationship with her mother.

She had failed where her mother had succeeded, and it drove them both crazy.

Suzanne went out the back door, locking it behind her, and climbed into her car. Gerry had done a showing a few miles outside of town at four o'clock and had said he was heading straight home afterward, and she had promised to close up shop for him.

Now it was time to go home.

Suzanne sighed, leaned her head against the steering wheel, and looked up ahead, toward the south and out of town, where she could just see the top of her mother's old house silhouetted against the purple twilight sky.

She really should get up there soon. The place needed a good clean, and there was something about the thermostat. Soon, she promised herself; not tonight, but soon.

She drove home, fixed a smile to her face, and went inside to start dinner.

CHAPTER SEVEN

Millie

The sun was shining when Millie woke up.

Bright, midday sun. December sun, she realized. It must be by now. Had she missed Thanksgiving? The thought shocked her. Thanksgiving had always been her favorite holiday.

She enjoyed spending the days leading up to it busy in the kitchen, her apron dusted with floury handprints.

The counters would be full of bowls and pans and baking sheets, the table heaped high with pies and cookies and candies.

She'd make such a mess that Arthur, bless him, would come into the kitchen and wash the dishes for her while she busily made more and more food.

In the old days, the really good old days, when the whole big family would come to spend Thanksgiving, they'd have to put all the leaves in the table in the formal dining room and pull all the chairs from their various places in the house, called back once again to their official use.

There were her and Arthur and the children, of course, plus her three younger siblings and their spouses, and a whole gaggle of little cousins to run and play together.

Those children would go laughing and shrieking through the house, and their mothers, congregated in the kitchen, would give them stern looks and shoo them out the back door to play in the cold November sunshine.

Of course, once the kids were out, the mothers would laugh, too.

They remembered well enough how it felt to be a child in this big old house, with its long hallways and mysterious rooms, its perfect hiding places.

Then they'd all gather around the table and feast, eating turkey and dressing and mashed potatoes, green beans and candied yams and dinner rolls, eating more and more till they all swore they couldn't eat any more, and then someone would always say, "But what about dessert?"

They would laugh and somehow find room in their full bellies for pumpkin pie and pecan pie, fudge and brownies and snickerdoodle cookies.

Those were good times. Happy times. But that was a long time ago.

The children had all grown up, as children do. They had moved away, spread across the country, married lovers of their own, had more children.

Except for her own children, of course. No grandchildren for her.

Millie's mouth tightened at the thought. She shook her head to force it away.

The children had scattered, and the Thanksgiving gatherings grew smaller and smaller until finally it was just Millie and Arthur, with Suzanne and Gerry driving up from town, and Mitch, when he could get away long enough, flying in for a few hours.

Eventually even flying in became too much trouble. By that time Mitch was working at a big fancy hospital in California, a *psychiatric health center* he called it.

But Millie knew what it really was. In her days they'd had their own name for it: the looney bin.

Mitch couldn't be gone from his precious health center for very long, it seemed. As if every patient in the place would riot and burn it to the ground if he were gone for a couple of days.

Millie had scoffed at him over the phone when he told her. And then she hung up and cried.

Then there had been four. Millie and Arthur, Suzanne and Gerry.

There was always too much then: too much food for just four people to eat, too much room at the table, even with none of the leaves put in, too much awkward silence where there should have been constant chatter.

And then there were three.

Arthur had died in January of 1993, and that year Suzanne had offered to have Thanksgiving at her house, so that her grieving mother wouldn't feel the need to put on a big production all on her own.

Millie had been offended at the idea but had kept her mouth shut, driving slowly down the hill and into town, parking in front of her daughter's ugly little split-level ranch, and chewing silently through tough turkey and lumpy potatoes.

She'd never had Thanksgiving dinner at Suzanne's again.

The memories that had started out so happy had now turned into a sour taste in Millie's mouth, a downturn of her lips. And now, apparently, she had completely missed an entire Thanksgiving, and her daughter didn't even care.

Well, she'd have a nice little celebration of her own. Yes, she felt like baking up something delicious. She'd make snickerdoodles. They were always Arthur's favorite, and *he* had really loved her, stuck by her till the Lord called him home.

She'd make them in honor of him.

So, Millie pulled bowls and spoons and measuring cups from the cabinets. Flour and eggs and sugar and cinnamon.

She spent the whole of the afternoon slowly making cookies.

Sometimes needed to sit and rest after one or two steps in the recipe she knew by heart, but she didn't mind. She didn't have anything else pressing her to do.

She had all the time in the world.

While the dough chilled in the fridge, she laid her head on her arms at the kitchen table and napped.

When she woke, the sun was setting, and pink light glowed against the western windows.

She warmed up the oven and slid in one, two, three batches of cookies, tracking the time on the old green clock mounted above the doorway.

Her arms were shaking by the time she pulled the last sheet of fragrant treats from the oven. Millie sat the final baking sheet down on the top of the stove, and she sampled one of the cookies from the first batch, the ones that had been sitting long enough to cool.

It was delicious.

She was exhausted. "Well, Arthur," she spoke in the direction of the ceiling, as if her husband was somewhere in the general direction of heaven, "I made these for you. Maybe you can at least smell them up there. I promise you they're tasty. And I miss you. Damn it, I miss you."

Her eyes clouded with tears, and she wiped them away, frustrated with herself.

She looked around at the mess in the kitchen. The counter was covered in cooling trays of cookies, the sink stacked with bowls and spoons to which clung bits of dough.

Bah. She was too tired to deal with it now. She'd come down and clean it in the morning.

She snatched two more cookies, placing one in each of the large front pockets of her dressing gown, and began the long journey down the hall, up the creaking stairs, and to bed.

She was so tired, but it was a good kind of tired. The kind you felt after a day of hard work.

She was asleep in seconds, the cookies forgotten in her pockets.

CHAPTER EIGHT

Millie

Standing at her front bedroom window, Millie could see the lights in the town below.

Houses were decked out in white, or red and green, or whole spectrums of colors. Trees appeared to be wrapped in rainbows.

Main Street was aglow with twinkling strands covering the buildings and zigzagging from rooftop to rooftop.

It was December for sure.

Millie hummed to herself as she straightened the quilts on her bed. She was feeling particularly sprightly this evening. Her internal rhythms had definitely gotten a bit off-kilter lately. She was practically a vampire!

The thought made her smile. She couldn't help it, though, her brain seemed to want to sleep through the daylight hours and drag itself to wakefulness a bit before sunset.

And who cared? She lived on her own time these days.

Still humming *on the fifth day of Christmas, my true love gave to me...* she crossed the upstairs hallway and peeked into Mitch's room. Would Mitch come home for Christmas this year?

She hoped so.

Oh! But she'd have to buy presents. Presents for Mitch and Suzanne and Suzanne's boyfriend, what was his name? Rocky! Mitch and Suzanne and Rocky.

No. Not Rocky. Rocky was before. Rocky was the bad one. It was Gerry now. Nice, sweet Gerry. Her husband, not her boyfriend. Wasn't he? Had they gotten married yet? Surely they had.

She hadn't missed the wedding, had she? No, no, she remembered the wedding. Down at the church. A modest affair.

Suzanne had worn white even though she was about as far from pure as you could get. Millie sighed. She had taught that girl better, really she had. But what can you do? Kids will be kids.

Kids. They were such good kids. So sweet, so fun, when they were little.

Mitch had tripped along from one obsession to another, from pirates to airplanes to cowboys to robots. Millie searched the shelves secured to the wall above Mitch's bed. Yes. There it was.

She stretched her arm as far she could above her head, raised her ancient body as far as it would go on her crooked toes.

She couldn't reach it.

Hiking up her nightgown, she climbed carefully, slowly, onto the bed. First on her knees, then, bracing herself against the wall, she stood on shaky legs. With one hand grasping the headboard, she stretched the other hand and could just reach the legs of the old metal robot, Mitch's favorite toy.

Her gnarled knuckles wrapped around it and pulled.

The robot, wheels hidden inside its feet, rolled forward more quickly than she'd anticipated. It was heavy, and as its weight came sliding off the shelf, Millie's other hand, the one that had been holding onto the bed, reached up to keep it from falling.

The robot fell.

Millie fell.

The robot hit the floor with a solid thud. Millie twisted as she dropped, and as she landed her feet were still on the bed, her body spilling down the side of it onto the floor, where her head thunked against the hardwood.

Her sparse white curls lay spread around her.

After a few minutes, a mouse came peeking out from under the bed to investigate. It sniffed around Millie's head, then cautiously scampered up the length of her body.

The mouse's tiny nose pushed into the pocket of her dressing gown, then the creature disappeared entirely into the pocket.

While Millie lay unconscious, the mouse, confused, sniffed and searched in the pockets which smelled of food but were completely empty.

CHAPTER NINE

Milllie

There was pain.

Dull, aching pain everywhere, and a sharper pain in her neck.

Millie's eyes fluttered open.

The room swam in and out of focus. Everything was wrong, and in her disorientation, it took Millie a few moments to realize that she was looking at the world upside down.

She could see the floor, the open door to the hallway beyond. Wooden legs of a desk. If she turned her head, the pain made her wince, but she could see something else.

The moonlight shone on the polished metal and red plastic eyes of Mitch's old toy robot.

It lay perhaps two feet away from her, in the center of the room.

Her left arm was flung out toward it. She stretched her fingers but could not reach it.

Mitch had received that robot as a Christmas present the year he turned nine.

He had been asking for it for months, and Millie and Arthur had told him it just wasn't in the budget that year. Then, over his disappointed head, they'd share that secret smile that only parents know.

Millie had wrapped the robot in shiny green paper with a big red bow, and she'd kept it hidden in the high cabinet over the washing machine.

On Christmas Eve, after the kids were asleep, she and Arthur had pulled all the presents from their varied hiding places and arranged them under the tree.

The box containing the robot had been placed far in the back, practically hidden.

When Christmas morning came and Mitch came bounding down the stairs at first light, with Suzanne trailing sleepily behind him, they'd started with the gifts in front.

One by one Mitch had torn open the paper wrappings, and though he liked the other presents, in his heart he'd still been dreaming, thinking that just maybe there was a chance that he would receive that most coveted toy.

As the pile of unopened presents grew ever smaller, his face couldn't hide his disappointment.

And then, when all his hope was lost, Arthur, sitting back on the couch, had said, "Why don't you look again, son, see if there's anything else?"

Mitch had ducked his head beneath the hanging boughs of the tree, squirmed his way into the back corner, and come out clutching the gift and scattering pine needles everywhere.

He had looked up at his parents with a cautious hope.

Off came the bow, Mitch's fingers slid into the slit where paper met paper, and he pulled it loose.

The moment he knew for certain what was inside, he'd let out a wild whoop and hugged the box to his chest. He'd rushed across the room and hugged both his parents in turn, gushing his *thank you* again and again.

When he had lifted the robot from the box his eyes shone with excitement. That was probably the happiest Millie had ever seen him.

She'd been lost there, for a moment, lost in a memory. Pain brought her back to the present.

She needed to move, but she wasn't sure if she could. There seemed to be no strength at all left in her body.

She turned her head back toward the desk. It was close enough, if she could just get her legs down off the bed, she could use the desk to prop herself upright, and from there she could try to stand, holding on to its sturdy weight.

She tried to swing her legs down off the bed. No good.

She tried to scoot herself backwards across the floor. Her progress was slow, but she was moving, one inch at a time.

After each push, she had to stop, rest, breathe. Her heart was pounding and so was her head.

It seemed an eternity passed before she finally pushed herself backward along the floor, like a turtle stranded on its shell, far enough that her legs slid off the bed and her feet hit the ground with a muffled bump.

More minutes ticked by as Millie shifted herself onto her side. Slowly, painfully, she got her elbows up onto the seat of the desk chair and hoisted herself into a sitting position on the floor.

She tried vainly to pull herself up to sit in the chair, or better yet, to stand beside the desk, but her aged muscles, atrophied with disuse, were not up to the challenge.

Her breath huffed and puffed through her lips as she shifted herself back down. She leaned her back against the desk, her legs spread out front of her on the floor.

She told herself she'd be okay. She'd get up eventually. She just needed to rest a bit, needed the room to stop spinning.

Her head ached, and she prodded gently at it with her fingers but couldn't feel a bump, and thankfully there didn't seem to be any blood.

She tried to take deep, calming breaths, in through her nose and out through her mouth. Her mouth was so dry, though. She needed a drink.

There was a cup sitting next to the sink in the bathroom, but that was all the way out of this room, down the hall a bit, and through another door.

She told herself not to think about it.

She leaned her head carefully against the desk and shut her eyes.

She felt her heartbeat slow and steady within her chest.

She heard the old house creak around her.

She heard the door open downstairs.

Her slow and steady heartbeat skipped a little. The dreamy fog that had been seeping into her mind pulled back. Her eyes fluttered open, and she listened. Footsteps. A flurry of quiet activity just at the bottom of the stairs.

Oh, thank God. It must be Suzanne. Suzanne had finally decided to show up for a visit. Or was it to clean? She had called and asked Suzanne to come help her clean, hadn't she?

She'd certainly meant to, and though she couldn't remember actually calling her daughter, she felt sure that must be why she was there.

Millie tried to call out to her daughter. Her voice was small and weak, breath rasping in her dry throat as she pushed the words out. Three times she called her daughter's name.

The door opened and slammed shut again.

Her daughter had left her. But no; Millie shook her head. Even in her state of half-delirium she knew that couldn't be true.

Suzanne wouldn't just come in for a few minutes and then leave. She'd look for her mother, and if she couldn't find her downstairs, she would go searching upstairs. Millie knew she would.

But if it hadn't been Suzanne coming in and going out, then who was it?

A bolt of fear shuddered through Millie's whole body as she heard the creak of footsteps on the stairs. The sound was both utterly familiar and completely terrifying.

The sixth stair up. She held her breath, waiting. And then it came: the thirteenth stair.

Whoever it was, they were coming up the stairs, and this meant they were currently just a few yards away.

This is how it ends, she thought, *a defenseless old woman attacked in her home, hooligans looking to loot and steal from the biggest house in town, with no scruples about quietly murdering the ancient lady who lived there.*

Resigned to her fate, and surprisingly calm about it, Millie waited.

After the creak of the stairs, there were no more sounds. She heard no footsteps coming down the hall toward the open door into Mitch's room. Her mind was contemplating the strange quiet when she felt it.

A feeling washed over her, an icy river that rushed through her marrow.

It felt for all the world like someone – or something – had come into the room with her. Millie barely dared to breathe.

She couldn't hear anything, couldn't see anything, unless, perhaps, the shadows in the corner there – the darkness against darkness – were they moving?

Yes, she swore there was movement around her, unseen and unheard but felt; wavers in the air, a disruption of the stillness.

In terror she watched as Mitch's old toy robot slowly raised until it stood upright and then… then it began to roll across the floor toward her.

Her veins seemed flooded with fear, coursing like poison through her body; goosebumps broke out over every inch of her, her heart pounded within her chest.

The robot stopped, inches from her foot. She didn't dare try to move. She didn't know if she could move, didn't know if her muscles, which had been betraying her so often lately, would obey the message her mind was trying to send.

The robot rolled slowly backward, away from her. Millie's eyes were wide in the darkness, her wrinkled hands clutching like talons at the front of her dressing gown.

The robot rolled forward again, and this time, as it came closer, fear-fueled adrenaline coursed through her from head to toe, and her muscles forgot their frozen weakness as she pushed herself up and against the desk, her hands grabbing first the chair and then the desktop, the solid old desk shaking beneath her frenzied attempt to get up and away from that impossible thing on the floor.

The robot stopped and so did Millie. Against all odds, she was upright, standing, her hands gripping the edge of the desk behind her as it dug into her spine. The robot's red eyes seemed to shine and blink at her in the darkness.

They were in a standoff, Millie and the robot, and with a shudder, Millie remembered the name Mitch had given to the robot all those years ago, on Christmas day, when the wrapping paper and bows had been cleared away and the breakfast dishes washed.

She remembered him looking up at her from this very floor as she stood in his doorway, remembered his broad smile, his little boy's voice:

"I named my robot, Mom. I named him Phantom."

As if it knew she remembered its name, the robot rolled slowly forward again. It was inching toward her slippers. A quiet sob escaped her, and she bit it back.

"No," she begged, though she didn't know if she was talking to robot or herself, to the memories crowding her head, or to whatever diabolic force was in her house, in this very room, with her,

"No, no, no, please no."

The robot stopped.

Millie stared at the toy. The toy stared back.

Seconds passed

The strength the adrenaline rush had lent to Millie's body began to fail, draining away and filling her instead with an alarming numbness. Her arms and legs shook.

She rested her weight against the bed at her back, slowly lowering herself a few inches until she could sit down.

The robot did not move.

The robot did not move, but something else did.

Millie could hear it, could hear the scrapes and shuffles, the small bumping and shifting that screamed to her mind that someone was right here in the room with her.

It came from the doorway, the closet, the window, a hundred tiny noises. Tears began to fall down Millie's face, dropping with tiny splashes onto her hands folded helplessly in her lap.

"Where are you?" she whispered.

"*What* are you? What do you want? Go away and leave me alone! Please, please just leave me alone."

Knock, knock.

A wailing sob ripped forth from deep inside her.

Knock, knock.

More quiet shifting and shuffling in the room.

Millie's breath seemed trapped inside her, her chest weighted down by terror.

Knock, knock.

She was trembling, shaking so badly that the entire bed moved beneath her and the headboard vibrated a sharp staccato against the wall: *tap tap tap tap tap*!

Knock.

Knock.

Knock.

With a wild shriek, Millie pushed off against the bed and rushed as quickly as she could out of the room.

Her back seized as she rose, and she shuffled, half bent, her slippered feet swooshing along the floor like a slow-motion ice skater.

She didn't stop until she reached the safety of her own bedroom, closing the door behind her and backing away from it slowly.

Was she safe here? She didn't know. What was out there, and could it open doors? Could it walk through doors? Could it… touch her?

Hurt her?

After waiting as long as her shaking legs would hold her up and hearing nothing else, Millie took a few steps to her bed.

She climbed in beneath the quilts and pulled them over her head like a small child frightened of the bogeyman. It seemed safer somehow beneath the layers of blankets, their heavy weight comforting.

Millie waited and listened.

And then she slept.

CHAPTER TEN

Mitch

Dr. Mitch Carver tried not to glance at his watch as he listened to his patient ramble on.

The patient – Jennifer – had been reluctant to speak when she'd first been admitted. She had progressed to slinging insults his way and cursing like a sailor after the first couple of weeks.

Now she had been here for almost two months and finally today the floodgates had opened. She was telling him about her childhood, and it was a doozy.

Mitch wasn't usually so preoccupied, but today he was doing something he hadn't done in many years; leaving work early was strange enough, but he was actually taking a vacation, which was practically unheard of.

He was supposed to leave at noon, but at last glance his watch had showed ten after.

He didn't want to stop Jennifer when she'd finally started talking, but at the same time, the schedule he had created for his day was going to be severely off if he didn't get moving soon.

He couldn't believe he was doing this in the first place.

Vacations were for people who were unhappy with their own lives, he'd always thought, and since he was quite happy with his, he'd really never had much use for them.

"It's not a *vacation*, Mitch," his sister Suzanne had scolded him over the phone a few days earlier.

"It's coming home for the holidays."

Mitch had sighed and agreed, grudgingly, to make the trek back to tiny Hillview, Missouri for a few days for Christmas.

In his mind he could picture the dark house at the top of the hill, the feeble yellow light from its windows.

His mother had refused to let him hire someone to update the wiring in the old place. He shook his head. *Stubborn old bat.*

"Doc? You here?" Jennifer's voice cut through his thoughts, "You seem to have drifted away a bit there, Doc."

Mitch realized with a pang of guilt that he truly had been lost in his own thoughts, and hadn't heard much of what Jennifer had been saying for the last – he checked his watch – ten minutes.

He glanced at his patient.

She wore standard issue pajamas, loose and comfortable, with a thick cardigan which she kept constantly wrapped tight around her like a defense against the world.

Her eyebrows were raised, and the corner of her mouth turned up in a smile.

"Geez, Doc, maybe you're the one needs your head examined," she proclaimed cockily.

Mitch shook his head and let out a sigh, admitting to them both that perhaps she was right.

"I'm sorry, Jennifer, my mind's not all here at the moment. Let's wrap this up and continue when I get back from my vacation."

Jennifer raised her eyebrows but didn't say anything. She shrugged and left the room.

Mitch waited a count of thirty to make sure she was well down the hallway before jolting into action.

He shut down his computer, put away his last files, tidied his desk. Briefcase in hand, he left the office, locking the door securely behind him, and hurried, head down, avoiding patients and nurses alike, down the endless corridors, through one heavy security door after another.

He smiled briefly and gave a wave to the receptionist in the sunny welcoming area, then burst out into the sunshine of a mild California winter.

It took Mitch half an hour to drive to his cozy little beach house, tucked away on two acres of private property. It took him another hour to pack all his things. He should have packed them earlier, the day before, he knew, but he'd honestly thought that he might get cold feet and change his mind about going right at the last moment, so he hadn't.

Now he carefully pulled shirts from their hangers in his massive closet, and placed them in his suitcase next to neatly folded pants and underwear, mated socks, and the comfy sweats and T-shirts he wore to sleep in.

He added a pair of nice but casual shoes, his toiletries, and finally his laptop.

He changed into jeans and an old sweatshirt and pulled on his most comfortable sneakers for the long drive ahead. His GPS told him it was a twenty-eight-hour trip, which he intended to spread out over three days.

With his suitcase in the trunk and his phone plugged into its spot on the dashboard, Mitch started the car and cranked up the music.

He drove to the end of his long private drive and then a thought occurred to him which made him turn around and drive back.

Suzanne had said there was work that needed doing on the old family home, and there was no telling if her ridiculous husband actually had any tools suitable for the job. Mitch sneered as he thought about it.

Why his sister had ever married that pale-faced pansy of a man, he would never know.

With his heavy toolbox now pushed in beside his suitcase, Mitch set off again. This time he didn't turn back.

CHAPTER ELEVEN

Suzanne

Suzanne moved dreamily from room to room in her spotless house.

She'd left work early, all the paperwork filed neatly, Gerry happily uploading pictures of their newest listing to the realty website.

There was nothing left for her to do there, and as long as someone was there just in case a new customer came in, all was good.

So Gerry was there, and she was here, at home, and that made her perfectly happy.

She had kicked off her shoes and changed into comfortable clothes the moment she'd come in, tiptoeing past the guest bedroom as though terrified of waking the old woman whose most precious belongings had been moved from the old house on the hill to this tiny room, a life packed up and transported.

She then poured herself a large glass of wine from the bottle in the fridge.

They didn't usually keep much alcohol in the house, but at the holiday season, having wine was practically required for Christmas parties and impromptu gatherings with friends who dropped by.

There were no friends there now, though, and Suzanne was glad of it.

She'd plugged her phone into the speakers in the living room and started up her Christmas playlist. Currently Bing Crosby was serenading her, and she swayed back and forth, the tiniest bit tipsy, in front of the large picture window that looked out over the front yard.

Bing was dreaming of a white Christmas and so was she. The probability of snow in December was roughly fifty-fifty in that part of the country, so she at least had a chance.

Surrounding her in the living room, stacked on the floor and on the furniture, were the boxes of Christmas decorations.

Gerry had brought them down from the tiny crawlspace that passed for an attic the night before.

Suzanne was home early on the pretense of beginning the decorating. She sighed and looked around. She knew she needed to get at least some of the work done before Gerry got home, or he would look at her with that queer little look in his eyes, that questioning tilt of his head, that suggested he knew there was a lot more going on in her head that she wasn't telling him.

He was right, of course. There always was.

It took her a few hours, but by four o'clock, she had emptied every box but one.

The empty boxes were stacked neatly in the hall, the house was aglow with Christmas lights, and her playlist had cycled through every song at least once.

Burl Ives was telling her to have a holly jolly Christmas as she sat down on the living room couch to open the last box.

She'd been saving this box for last, or putting it off, if she was really honest with herself. These were the heirloom decorations, the ones that had been her mother's, her grandmother's, and beyond.

She lifted the lid from the box reverently.

From the top she pulled out two porcelain figures, each perhaps eight inches tall. The Nutcracker and the Mouse King.

She dug carefully through the tissue paper packing and pulled out the third in the set: Clara in her nightgown.

Suzanne smiled, a smile that held sadness as much as joy, as she remembered those beautiful hazy childhood Christmases tucked away in her mind.

She'd been eight years old, bouncing up and down in her pink leotard and tights, as she and her mother had checked the cast sheet.

Her mother had warned her not to get her hopes up, that it was possible she wouldn't get a part, but her name had been there after all: Suzanne Carver – Mouse.

Her mother had, of course, been disappointed. She'd wanted her daughter to have a bigger part, possibly; a more feminine part, surely.

But Suzanne hadn't cared. She was happy to wear a gray costume and don her mouse-ear headband, pinned so tightly to her head that it felt as if the bobby pins were scraping right through into her skull.

There had been eight weeks of rehearsals and then three glorious nights of performance.

Her parents had been there every single night, and every night her father had presented her with a bouquet of pink roses.

He'd hugged her and tossed her in the air and laughed and told her what a wonderful job she had done, that surely she was the best little mouse dancer ever to grace any stage the whole world over.

Her mother had nodded and granted her a tight smile.

That same year the porcelain Nutcracker figures had appeared on the fireplace mantle, whisked there by the Sugar Plum Fairy herself, according to Suzanne's father, as he winked his eye and put a finger to his lips to show that this was a special secret between father and daughter.

Of course she knew that, really, he'd bought them himself, knew that her mother had not known he was doing it by the look of surprise on her face when she came home from her meeting at the church and saw them standing in pride of place on the parlor mantel.

The wine soured in Suzanne's stomach now as she remembered the day she had packed this box up.

The look on her mother's face.

Suzanne had been honestly surprised when her mother had asked that she search through the boxes of decorations up at the old house and find the special pieces, the antiques and the ones with significant memories attached to them.

Her mother had sat in her favorite chair in the parlor, watching like a hawk as Suzanne shifted gently through the boxes, setting aside swags of tinsel and strings of lights which probably didn't even work anymore.

Each time Suzanne had pulled out one of the special items, wrapped it carefully in tissue paper, and placed it in the keepsake box, her mother had sucked in a sharp breath, stiffening in her seat.

"Mother, are you sure you want me to do this right now?" Suzanne had asked.

Her mother had sighed, that way she had of sighing that told you exactly how disappointing you were.

"Yes. I'd rather it gets done now while I can see that it's done properly. I'm old, you know. And since I won't be decorating here at the family home anymore," – another sigh – "these things might as well be put with your own decorations," her mother had said.

"Though who knows who they'll go to once you're dead and gone yourself."

Her mother had then taking to mumbling to herself while Suzanne did her best to tune her out and finish the packing.

Suzanne's eyes had clouded with tears as she caught snatches of her mother's words: *no grandchildren to pass things on to; no one left to live in the grand old house on top of the hill; no legacy for her, no, her branch would be lopped off the family tree, dead and shriveled.*

Suzanne had done her best to ignore the words, to deflect the barbs flung in her direction. Her mother was getting old, and possibly senile.

She'd been complaining lately of things that couldn't possibly be happening: noises in the house that her had convinced someone was in there every night trying to rob her, or kill her, or worse – though Suzanne couldn't imagine what was supposedly worse.

Lights going off and on by themselves. That sort of thing.

Suzanne was sure that everything was in her mother's head. She and Gerry had checked the entire house over, and nothing was missing or out of place, every door and window securely locked.

That was when they'd started discussing moving her mother in with them.

Sitting in the living room, mind fogged with wine, Suzanne's eyes drifted to the stairs, thinking of the room beyond that they had prepared for her mother.

It had been one of the hardest things she'd ever done; this was largely, guiltily, because she hadn't wanted her mother to be anywhere near her.

A car horn honked outside, and lights flashed across the window.

Quickly Suzanne wrapped the figurines back in their tissue and packed them away.

She slid the box back into the corner behind the couch and stood, smoothing back her hair and practicing her smile, as Gerry's keys jingled in the front door lock.

CHAPTER TWELVE

Millie

Millie shivered in the darkness.

The only warmth came from a pocket of air around her head where her own hot breath bounced back into her face.

The rest of her body felt like ice.

She opened her eyes in the darkness. She was in bed. A shaft of silvery moonlight shone in through the crack in the drapes. Her quilts lay in a tangled heap at the foot of the bed, spilling off the bed like a patchwork waterfall and puddling on the floor below.

Stiff with cold and age, Millie struggled with the blankets, finally managing to pull them back up onto the bed and tucking them around her like a cocoon.

She lay back against the pillows.

Movement beyond the window made her stir, suddenly afraid, but then she smiled.

Just a flurry of snowflakes picked up in a gust of wind and swirling beyond the glass.

Snow.

Her smile widened as her body slowed its shaking beneath the quilts. She loved snow. Perhaps they'd have a white Christmas after all.

She could hear a sound now, the wind whistling against the eaves, howling around the corners of the old house. The world beyond her window seemed nothing but a two-inch gap of black sky and whirling white.

Millie hummed to herself, the tuneless notes vibrating in her throat transformed in her mind to the voice of old Bing Crosby. He had been quite the crooner, old Bing. Ugly as sin, she knew, but oh, that voice.

It was always the first record she'd put on the Victrola each year at Christmastime, when the children were young and happy, eyes shining as the decorations went up and their father came home dragging a Christmas tree cut down in the woods beyond the house, hopeful for presents and eating cookies and candy from the kitchen as fast as Millie could make them.

Millie's mind drifted down the years, weaving in and out of holiday feasts, late night gift wrapping, swanky parties with she and Arthur and their friends dressed in red and green and gold, sipping spiked eggnog and laughing.

Further and further back her mind traveled, all the way to her own childhood Christmases, leaner than perhaps they would normally have been, there in the midst of the hardship that would later be called the Great Depression.

But they hadn't been depressed, not really, not the children. They hadn't known that those years in the 1930s had produced less gifts than they might have, hadn't realized there ever could have been more, and therefore hadn't missed it.

They had been happy.

Her father had grown up wealthy and would have been hopelessly lost without her mother.

Helen Carver had certainly not grown up well-off, and she knew how to balance a tight budget, pinch the pennies, ration out the meager food supplies so that they lasted.

She had known how to patch up the holes in the boys' trouser knees and how to cut more fabric for a dress than necessary, hemming it at first and letting the hem out little by little so that it lasted for two or three years, even on a gangly ten-year-old girl.

Millie's fingers caressed her covering of quilts gently, reverently.

Of course when the clothes – or the sheets, or the drapes, or the flour sacks – had been beyond suitability for standard use, her mother had cut them into scraps and made quilts, lining the insides with older blankets that were losing their strength, and while sitting in the kitchen rocking chair in the evenings, she'd make the most beautiful, warm coverings for her family's beds.

Every quilt that lay, even now, on Millie's bed, had been made by her mother.

At the bottom of the pile lay Millie's wedding quilt, which her mother had crafted from real store-bought fabric off the bolt, and on top of that lay two of the patchwork quilts that held a hundred memories of Sunday dresses and starched shirts and flowery nightgowns.

Once upon a time, Millie had been able to remember where many of the small squares of fabric came from, but now, like so many other things, those memories had flown away somewhere, or been tucked so deeply under a lifetime of days that she could no longer recall them.

Millie sighed, a loss and a yearning for happier times carried away on her breath.

Her body had stopped its violent shivering, but she was still cold.

Running her hands up inside the sleeves of her dressing gown, she could feel the coolness of her own papery skin. It was cold in the house.

She'd have to go check that blasted thermostat again. And she'd have to be more forceful when demanding that Suzanne get Gerry or somebody up here to fix it.

She considered wrapping one of the quilts around her as she made her way downstairs but decided against it. That seemed like a disastrous accident waiting to happen, an old woman tangled up in her own blankets, losing her balance and tumbling headfirst down the stairs.

The thought gripped her suddenly, the scene playing out in shocking realism before her eyes, her body tensing up at the anticipated pain of her body bruised and broken.

Millie shook her head to rid herself of the image, gripped the banister tightly, and made her way down the stairs slowly and carefully, counting as she went and nodding approvingly at the creaks on the third and tenth stairs.

A shudder ran through her as she stepped down into the front hallway. It was even colder downstairs that it had been up in her bedroom.

She shuffled to the thermostat. No wonder it was so cold, the damn thing was on the blink again. She turned the dial in the darkness, listened as the heater clicked and hummed.

Satisfied, she made her way to the kitchen for a cup of hot tea.

She stopped when she entered the kitchen, confused.

Things were not right in here at all.

A stack of her best mixing bowls sat on the counter next to the sink, the handle of a wooden spoon sticking out of the top one. Millie stood in the doorway, regarding this out of place oddity with suspicious eyes.

And that wasn't all. She could have just been imagining it, but she could swear that the kitchen table wasn't in its proper place. It wasn't an obvious change; the table was simply about three inches further to her right than it should have been.

That table had sat in the same spot in that kitchen for fifty years at least, and now it had been moved. Yes, she was sure of it.

Had Suzanne done this? Suzanne *had* been here, hadn't she?

Millie had a vague recollection of Suzanne coming in the front door. She had called and asked her to come, hadn't she? To do a bit of cleaning?

Well, if this was Suzanne's idea of cleaning, leaving dishes stacked on the countertops instead of put away neatly in the cabinet where they belonged, and moving around the furniture as if her mother wouldn't notice, that girl needed a talking-to.

Millie would surely give her a piece of her mind next time she spoke to her. For now, though, she would put her kitchen back to rights.

Millie pushed against the table with her hands. It wouldn't budge. She didn't remember it ever being this heavy.

She pushed again, leaning into the table with her hip and putting all her feeble strength into the motion. The table moved perhaps an inch.

She waited, caught her breath, tried again.

This time the table lurched another two inches across the floor, nearly making her tumble over as she slid along with it.

Regaining her balance, she backed up to look around once more. The table was back in its proper place.

But there…

It took a moment for her mind to catch up to what her eyes had just seen. There, in the doorway leading out to the hallway, a person was standing, a shadowy figure in the darkness.

Millie screamed.

She blinked.

The figure was gone.

Shaking, she lowered herself into the chair beside the kitchen table. There was a strange warmth to the chair, as if someone else had been sitting there just moments before, their body heat held in the grain of the wood.

As she sat, the warmth seemed to rise, wave upon wave passing over her, spreading up to her face and down to her feet at the same time.

It felt strangely pleasant.

Millie let the warmth envelop her. She didn't understand it but it was a welcome feeling just the same. She laid her arms on the table, her head on her arms.

Knock, knock.

It was quieter this time, and yet closer.

Knock.

Millie could feel the vibration of the sound coming up through the wood of the table. She lifted her head but pressed her palms flat against the tabletop.

Knock, knock.

Holding her breath, her body tense, Millie lifted her right hand and rapped her knuckles gently on the wood: knock, knock.

The heat surrounding her seemed to grow.

The response came louder this time.

Knock. Knock knock.

Firmly Millie knocked back: knock, knock-knock.

For several minutes the knocking continued. The ghost – spirit – entity – whatever it was, would knock against the table.

One knock, two, sometimes three. Millie could feel a presence around her, like someone standing a bit to the side and behind her, a form just beyond the edges of her vision.

Millie would knock back.

Each time she knocked, the heat would flare again, a slight shimmer in the air that made her think of long car rides across the desert in the heat of summer, a warmth that melted away the chill in her old bones.

Millie's mind was strangely calm. She did not feel that this presence wanted to hurt her.

She wondered, suspected, hoped even that it might be the spirit of her long-lost brother Davey, or perhaps the love of her life, Arthur, come back to chase away her loneliness in these long, dark days of her old age.

Her voice came out quiet, creaky, through vocal cords grown rusty from lack of use.

"Davey?" she called, "Arthur? Is it you?

A knock sounded loudly against the table.

Louder, she called, "Arthur? Are you there, Arthur?"

Like a jolt of electricity, something seemed to pass forcefully through Millie's body, a shot that rose up and away in the space of a second.

Immediately the warmth left her and the cold flooded back into her body. Her breath caught in her throat; jumbled thoughts tumbled around in her mind.

Was it Arthur?

She had thought, for a moment, that it must be, but the sudden violent departure of the cocooning warmth had startled her, and that didn't seem like Arthur at all.

Quietly this time, her voice a rasping whisper, she asked again.

"Arthur?"

She peered around the room, squinting her eyes against the light, trying to discern any ghostly signs of her beloved husband.

Again, there in the dim light of the hallway, a shadow seemed to emerge, a blurred outline of a person, a pencil shading against black paper. Millie stood, holding the table to steady herself.

The shadow moved. It stepped toward her; once, twice. Millie's legs tangled against each other, the chair behind her falling against the floor with a loud thud.

She turned quickly, and just as quickly lurched away to the right, as her eyes took in another shadowy shape, this one towering at least a foot above her, standing directly behind her.

She let out a series of small mouse-like squeaks, tiny, frightened noises that she could not control as she cowered against the kitchen sink.

The two shadows became three, then four; four faceless columns of gray fog in the vague shape of people, surrounding her there in her own kitchen.

She looked to her possible exits as her heart pounded and her blood thundered in her ears. Two shadows stood between her and the doorway to the hall, two others stood in the way of the back door. Her only other possibility of escape was the door to the basement, but even then she'd only be trapping herself with nowhere else to go.

Panicking, she lunged for the basement door, shaking the doorknob furiously before finally her mind screamed at her: *the locks!*

Fumbling with the locks, stinging pain as she tore part of a fingernail in the struggle, one lock slid back – *clank!* – the second lock slid back – *clink!* – and she was pulling the door open, creaking on its rusty hinges.

Then she was through the door, pulling it fast shut behind her, glimpsing as she did the shadowy figures still motionless in the kitchen.

She stood, leaning against the old stone walls, the doorknob gripped tightly in her hands. There was no lock on this side but she intended to use all her strength to keep the door held shut.

But what if – what if they could simply come through the door? What if doors and walls were no obstacle to those things out there?

Tears ran down her face; fear and frustration bubbled inside her.

That was *not* Arthur, that was… she didn't know what it was but it certainly didn't feel friendly and warm now.

She waited, shivering, arthritis sending shooting pains up her arms as she held fast to the doorknob, listening, straining her ears against the silence and her eyes against the darkness.

Were they still out there, whatever they were? Would they hurt her? *Could* they hurt her?

She knew she couldn't stay here forever, not even for long. The chill in the basement was worse than in the main part of the house, it was pitch black, and her poor old body was already beginning to shake with fatigue.

Even if the stairs behind her weren't a path to a cold trap, she didn't trust herself to navigate them in the dark, with muscles and bones that were unreliable even in the best of times.

Carefully, she released her grip on the knob and leaned her ear against the door. Were there movements, whisperings on the other side of the wood, or was that just the sound of her own blood rushing through her ears?

She took deep breaths, trying to calm her racing heart, and listened.

KNOCK KNOCK!

The sound came, loudly, from the other side of the door.

A small cry from Millie as she stumbled backward.

The scrape of feet against wood, nails against stone.

The creaking and banging of something heavy going ungracefully down the stairs.

A final, muffled thump in the darkness.

Then silence.

Silence, and cold.

CHAPTER THIRTEEN

Suzanne

Suzanne paced nervously, back and forth in front of the picture window.

The world outside was beautiful, a true winter wonderland: clean, white snow covering the ground and perched precariously along every branch of every tree, colored lights on all the houses shining bright in the falling darkness.

It was a perfect picture of lovely serenity but looking out at it did nothing to calm Suzanne's nerves, which were anything but peaceful.

Her brother, Mitch, would be here soon.

He'd left his home on the West Coast three days ago, driving the infamous Route 66 all the way from southern California to Missouri, exiting just a bit before the highway hit St Louis, taking the smaller roads home to Hillview.

She should be excited, she knew, and she was, a little. Mitch hadn't been home for Christmas in years, and even then it had been a rare treat.

Of course it hadn't *always* been a treat. Suzanne and her brother could be civil long enough, leave the touchy, sensitive subjects alone long enough, to enjoy a couple of days together, laughing over happy memories and avoiding the troubling ones by unspoken agreement.

But their mother in her later years had lost all sense of tact and subtlety; she had simply stopped caring if the things she said hurt other people.

It was their mother that had driven Mitch away to begin with. He'd never said as much, but Suzanne knew it was true.

If she was honest with herself, it was their mother who had driven her away all those years ago as well. The difference between Mitch and herself was that he had been smart about his running away: college scholarships, hard work, late nights studying, and a relentless ambition had led him to a respected title, a well-paying job, and a ridiculously expensive house on the beach.

Suzanne knew how much he'd paid for that house, she'd looked it up by the MLS number and sat, open mouthed, staring at the price tag.

Suzanne had taken a wilder, more reckless approach to getting away from her mother.

Her desire had been every bit as strong as Mitch's, but her foresight and planning had been pretty much nonexistent.

She'd been swept along on a wave of emotion and desperation. And then the tide that washed her out and away from Hillview had come rushing back in, carrying her helplessly along with it.

And now here she was, in her own house with her own husband, all those things her mother had wanted for her, and yet nobody was truly happy with the way things had turned out.

Gerry had gone to bed at nine-thirty, claiming a headache.

Suzanne knew he didn't really have a headache, or if he did it was only because he had given himself one by thinking about Mitch's arrival.

But she was happy enough to have him tucked up in bed, with the whole rest of the house to herself as she waited for her brother.

Christmas was only five days away.

There was a tasteful display of prettily wrapped gifts below the tree, but none for Mitch.

"Just promise me no gifts, Suze," he'd said over the phone, and she'd been relieved to hear it.

What did you buy a brother you barely knew any more, a rich man who already seemed to have everything he wanted?

Suzanne hated calling her brother on the phone. If she called him during the day, he always seemed irritated that she'd interrupted his oh-so-important work.

If she called him in the evenings or on Sundays when they were both free from work, Gerry would sit, half-listening to the conversation, rolling his eyes and sighing. Gerry was getting rather like her mother, in that way, now that she thought about it.

The phone calls were never about pleasant things anyway. It was always something about their mother, some new issue to deal with, some new tragedy that had befallen her or the old creaking house on the hill.

Suzanne was always the one that really had to deal with these things, the one whom the weight of decisions and work fell upon, but she still liked to keep Mitch informed, get his opinion, feel like she had his support backing her up when she went to deal with whatever difficulties had arisen.

Suzanne poured herself another glass of wine, made herself sit for a few moments, her body angled so she could see the moment Mitch's car came down the street.

She thought of the last ten years, of all the phone calls she'd had to make, all the strain between herself and her brother, herself and her mother.

There'd been a call when their mother practically stopped eating altogether (*just keep an eye on her, Suze, she probably doesn't need many calories these days*).

A call when their mother started losing bits of her short term memory (*just play along with her, Suze, that's normal in someone her age, who cares if she can remember what she ate for breakfast yesterday*).

A call when their mother started sleeping through the days, always snoring softly in her bed or her favorite chair in the parlor when Suzanne went to visit, only awake when the sun went down, awake all alone in the night up there on the hill (*so what, Suze, she's become a night owl in her old age, it won't hurt anything*).

A call when her mother's mind had really started to slip, when she became so lost in her own mind, in her memories, that she talked to people long dead – her brother, her mother, her husband – like they were still there in the room with her (*a pause on the line, a hint of concern finally creeping into his voice: yes, that might be a little concerning, Suze, let me think about it.*)

A call when Suzanne and Gerry had talked it over and decided that they would have to move Mother into their guest room, that she was too old and senile to care for herself properly anymore (*well, Suze, if that's what you think is best I won't stop you... no, I can't really get away right now to come help you move her, sorry.*)

And of course, the last call. The one Suzanne had made with shaking hands.

The call to Mitch as soon as she'd hung up from talking to the 911 dispatcher. The call after she'd gone up to check on their mother, to pack up a few more of her things before they moved her on the weekend, and had gone through the house, looking for her, calling out her name.

The memory now made Suzanne shiver and wrap her arms tightly around herself. The door to the basement, firmly shut, but unlocked.

The locks sitting, useless, their bolts slid back against the door. She'd stared at them, horrified, for the briefest moment, before she'd flung the door open and hurried down the rickety wooden steps as fast as she dared.

That phone call, after she'd found her mother's body, little more than a lump on the concrete at the bottom of the stairs. The faintest pulse had beat in her mother's neck as she'd pressed her fingers against it, a moan barely more than a whisper slipping out between her mother's lips as Suzanne cradled her head in her lap and dialed her phone.

Of course that phone call had gotten Mitch moving. Finally.

Suzanne shook her head and smiled a sad smile. Even when he'd gotten up and going, he'd been so long in coming that their mother hadn't even been in the hospital anymore.

It was Suzanne who had sat in the small, cramped room, watching as the machines pumped life into the frail old body lying motionless on the bed.

It was Suzanne, of course, who had taken care of everything, who had finally brought her mother home. Home, if she could call it that.

She glanced sharply up toward the small bedroom at the top of the stairs. The door remained closed. Home was where the heart was, she supposed, but she wasn't sure anybody's heart was really in this house.

But all that was in the past, water under the bridge, and now she had convinced Mitch to come home for the holidays.

Mother would want it, she had pointed out sternly, and she had practically heard the eye roll as his sigh came over the phone line. She had begged and lectured and finally broken down her brother's resolve, and now the family would be together for Christmas.

Well, what tiny bit of the family was left, anyway.

CHAPTER FOURTEEN

Mitch & Suzanne

Mitch pulled into his sister's driveway and stared at the house.

Married to the only realtor for fifty miles, and still she managed to live in one of the ugliest houses in town.

He loved his sister, but her pathetic little life made him angry. Angry at her for settling, angry at himself for not helping her, angry most of all at their mother, because really everything seemed to come back to her in the end.

He chuckled; Freud would have a field day with this family.

He took his suitcase with him up to the front door. His hand paused, fingers curled into a knocking fist, inches from the wood. He was looking in through the large picture window that stretched across the front of the house.

Inside the house all was glowing and peaceful, a lighted tree in one corner, candles and pine swags and tiny reindeer everywhere you looked. It seemed like a happy place.

Mitch knew better.

The moment his fist touched the wood – *knock, knock* – the door swung open, as if Suzanne had been standing just on the other side, waiting for him to announce his presence.

For a few seconds they stood looking at each other, then Suzanne smiled a tentative smile. Mitch laughed, shrugged. Suzanne held out her arms and they hugged, awkward and uncomfortable.

Suzanne ushered him in and closed the door behind him, shutting out the cold and darkness and welcoming him into the warmth and light of her happy *miserable* little home.

She showed him upstairs to the smaller of the guest rooms, shaking her head when his eyes looked to the other room, the one which had been so lovely before but was now taken over with their mother's boxed up life.

She put a finger to her lips. Not tonight, they'd leave that hornet's nest to be disturbed tomorrow.

Mitch looked around the small room he was presented with. It was drab and boring and at least fifteen years out of style but it would be well enough, he supposed, for a place to sleep for a few nights.

He laid his suitcase across the bed and turned to close the door. Suzanne was standing in the way, leaning against the door frame, smiling hopefully.

"I've got fresh cookies downstairs, and… and milk? Or hot chocolate?" she offered.

Mitch just stared at her.

"Or…something stronger?" Her voice was whining, begging.

Mitch took a firm stance, hand on the door.

"Not tonight, Suze. I've been driving for hours. I just want to get some sleep."

His sister's face fell at the words, eyes downcast, mouth frowning. Mitch sighed.

"Tomorrow, Suze. We can talk and start dealing with all this stuff with Mother tomorrow and… and have cookies."

Suzanne nodded silently and stepped back as Mitch closed the door. She shouldn't have expected any better, she knew, but she had hoped. She didn't know why. Hope had never done her any good.

The house was quiet around her.

Gerry was sound asleep by now. Even Mitch, in a room just a few steps away from her, must have been tiptoeing around as he prepared for bed, or perhaps standing there, just as she was, each of them waiting to hear what the other would do next.

Only the steady hum of the heater moved the air.

Suzanne took a deep breath, wiped away the tears that had gathered in pools along her lower eyelids, and went downstairs to turn out all the lights.

CHAPTER FIFTEEN

Suzanne & Mitch

Suzanne was waiting for Mitch when he came down the stairs the next morning.

She had changed her clothes, her hair was brushed and swept back from her face in a long ponytail, but the skin around her eyes was dark and puffy and Mitch suspected that she'd been up most of the night crying.

She offered him a cup of coffee, a peace offering in a Christmas mug. He took it and sipped at the hot liquid.

"Gerry says he can handle the office today, so I can stay here, and we can… we can do whatever…" Suzanne's mouth trembled its way into half a smile.

Mitch felt a mixture of pity and revulsion for her, for this whole place, this house, this town, this family. He figured he might as well cut to the chase, get things over with.

"I want to go up to the old house today," he said, blowing across the top of his coffee. "See what kind of state the place is in."

Suzanne looked uncomfortable at this suggestion.

"I thought you might like to visit Mother today," she said.

Mitch stared at her for a moment. "Later, maybe. Right now, I want to see the house."

Suzanne opened her mouth, shut it. Her shoulders slumped in resignation. She pasted a tight-lipped smile on her face and agreed.

Mitch was already out the door and headed up to the family home in his own car before Suzanne had gathered her things to follow him.

She supposed he didn't want to be stuck in the close proximity to her that a shared car ride would require. She knew that shouldn't surprise her.

She stood in the doorway for a few moments, watching the road out of town, spotting his car as it started up the hill. She thought it might be good to give him a few minutes alone at the house before she pulled up.

Mitch parked his car in front of his childhood home and got out. He stood, leaning against the car, looking up at it.

The paint was peeling all around. One of the upstairs shutters had fallen off and was lying on the ground in a pile of leaves. More leaves covered the large front porch.

The drapes were all drawn tightly closed, the windows like blank black holes across the front of the house.

As Mitch let his eyes drift upward, a slight movement caught his eye.

He stood up straighter and tilted his head, peering up at the window where he'd seen something, though he wasn't sure what. Had the drapes moved? But they couldn't have, could they?

It took his mind a beat or two to realize that the window he was staring at was one of the windows of his parents' bedroom. A shiver passed through his body. He laughed out loud.

He was a grown man, standing in front of a house, thinking he saw movement. What did he think it was, a ghost? He laughed again.

No, he knew this house was about as dead as it could be. Not even a ghost - if he believed in such things – would want to hang around here. He knew that whatever he'd seen had probably just been a trick of the morning light, or maybe a squirrel that had darted in front of the window and disappeared out of sight around the corner just as he glanced up.

Maybe it actually was that the drapes had moved; it wouldn't have surprised him at all to find a broken window somewhere around the back of the house, letting in just enough wind to stir the air in one of the front rooms.

Mitch opened his trunk to retrieve his toolbox. He sat it on top of the car while he rummaged around in his pockets for his keys.

The sun glinted dully off the tarnished brass plaque screwed to the front of the toolbox: *Property of Arthur Carver*.

The toolbox had been one of the few things Mitch had cared to have of his father's. He'd taken it home with him after the funeral, almost thirty years ago.

He could remember that drive like it was yesterday.

He'd placed the toolbox in the passenger seat of his car, and through the long drive home, he'd talked to it, glanced at it, run his hand along the worn surface of it.

For three days of driving it had stood in for the father he'd lost, and he'd released his grief through talk of baseball and hockey, fishing and car repair, old memories and the new things happening in his life.

He'd even brought the toolbox into his motel room with him each night and had set it on the small table next to the bed, a close, comforting presence as he went to sleep.

Mitch was surprised to find tears rolling down his face even now as he stood in the December sunshine.

The air was cold and there were clouds far off to the west that might spell rain, or maybe even snow, later in the day, but right now the sun was bright, and the wind was still.

Mitch took in several deep cleansing breaths.

Suzanne's car pulled into the drive.

Mitch unlocked the front door and entered the house, his sister coming up the stairs behind him.

A few curled leaves drifted in and scuttled across the floor of the entry hall.

The house was dim. Mitch shivered in the chilled air. He flicked the light switch. The overhead light flickered, then slowly steadied and rose to a sad yellow glow.

Mitch went quickly then, through the entire downstairs, flipping lights on. He peered at the hallway thermostat in the gloom, then rotated the dial and listened for the sound of the heater kicking on.

If he was going to be doing work in the house for a day or two, he certainly didn't intend to freeze to death while he did it.

The rooms had the feel of space long abandoned. A layer of dust covered everything in sight. Mitch ran his hand along the desk in the old office and grimaced at the gray smudge it left on his fingertips. Did Suzanne never clean the place?

"Suze?" He turned to speak to her, but she wasn't in the room.

Walking back out into the hallway, he saw her still standing in the entry way, looking up the stairs to the second floor.

Her face seemed pale and her hands twisted together nervously in front of her.

"Suze?" Mitch stopped next to his sister and followed her line of sight up the stairs.

All he saw was the walls and doors of the upstairs hall.

"Suze!"

He grasped Suzanne's arm and shook her gently.

"Oh!" she cried, and then laughed a little.

"Sorry, I just… I thought I heard…"

Her eyes drifted back to the stairs. Mitch stepped directly in front of her, blocking her view.

"Heard what, Suze?"

She laughed again, a tremulous little twitter that made her sound like an old woman.

"Nothing, nothing, really, don't worry about it."

Mitch looked into her eyes, concern furrowing his brow. He was looking at her like he thought she might be crazy, and the thought made her laugh again.

In truth it wasn't "nothing at all," in truth she had heard what sounded like the creaking of the stairs, as if someone had just gone up ahead of her and disappeared down the long dark hallway above.

But she knew that couldn't be true.

She also knew something that Mitch didn't. In the last few weeks before the accident, before their mother had fallen down the basement stairs, she'd been acting very strangely.

When Suzanne came to check on her, their mother had often not quite been there. She'd acted as if she wasn't even aware that Suzanne was in the room sometimes and had talked to people long dead as if they were sitting right next to her.

Memories had morphed into ghosts inside her mother's head, and far in the back of her own mind, Suzanne had begun to wonder if perhaps her mother had willed the memories into some kind of physical existence here in this lonely old house.

It was silly, she knew, crazy even, but there was something about the house that bothered her now, a feeling more than anything, a discomfort, a displacement, a gnawing edge of fear that someone was always there with her, just one step behind her, and if she could turn fast enough she'd catch a glimpse of them.

But she never did turn fast enough.

It was those feelings, those creeping goosebumps along her arms, that had caused her to do something even she couldn't believe.

"Suzanne!"

Mitch's voice came from the kitchen, an angry note threaded through it.

She half-ran down the hallway. Mitch was standing near the old table where their mother would sit to chop vegetables or shell peas.

His hand was perched, fingers tented up, over a piece of paper lying on the table. Suzanne walked closer and turned her head to see what it was he had found. Across the top of the paper an official letterhead proclaimed:

HILLVIEW PARANORMAL RESEARCH TEAM

Beneath the letterhead were some words scrawled in blue ink, what seemed to be a date and times, words written in some sort of messy shorthand or code that Suzanne couldn't quite decipher.

Mitch was fuming as he spoke. "What the hell is this?"

Suzanne stood there, speechless, her mind weighing her options.

Lie to her brother, tell him she didn't know where the paper had come from? Tell the truth, that she'd hired a paranormal research team – ghost hunters – to investigate the house, weeks ago?

If she lied, he'd just find out the truth anyway.

It would only take one phone call to the team – their name was right there on the paper; the number wouldn't be hard for him to find – and they'd tell him the truth themselves. So, better to just get it over with now.

She told him everything.

How their mother had acted during her last few months in the house, how she'd talked to people who weren't there, complained of things being moved in the night, lights turned on, strange noises in the house.

Mitch dismissed these things all as the result of their mother's age, her mind straying from reality, living in the past, forgetting things in the present. Suzanne knew this;

she wasn't stupid, and she told him so. She had thought the same thing at first, but then…

When their mother had been in the hospital after her fall down the basement stairs, Suzanne had come back to the house, alone, just as the sun had set, to gather up the rest of her mother's personal things.

She had known then that her mother would never return to live in this house, would never again roam, lonely and confused, through its dim hallways and shadowy rooms.

And as she had gone through her mother's things, selecting the items to take with her, she had felt a creeping dread make its way up her spine, an icy cold curling up and settling at the back of her neck.

The feeling had spooked her so much she'd practically run from the house.

And every time she'd been back to the house since then, things had been even stranger.

Cold spots, floors creaking, lights turned on when she knew she'd left the house in darkness the last time she'd been there, the thermostat settings changed, distant snatches of music.

It was enough to convince her that maybe their mother hadn't been imagining these things, maybe there really was something supernatural in this house.

And so, when she'd seen a flyer for the local ghost hunting group on the bulletin board at the library, she'd acted.

Mitch stood listening to all of this, disbelief narrowing his eyes and pinching his lips. He had known his mother was losing her grip on reality; he'd had no idea his sister was as well. He was shocked, he was dumbfounded, and he was angry.

"You invited a group of total strangers into this house?" Mitch's voice rose little by little as he spoke.

"You just handed over the keys to a bunch of crackpot ghost hunters? There's no telling what damage they've done to the house! What they've stolen!"

Mitch's face was growing red, spittle flying from his lips as he berated his sister, told her how ridiculous the whole thing was, how crazy it was to even believe that there were ghosts in the house, how completely stupid she was for giving people she didn't even know – and people who claimed to be ghost hunters, which meant they were either scam artists or just as crazy as she was – unsupervised access to their mother's house.

Suzanne shrank back against the kitchen counter, covered her face with her hands, and swallowed down the sobs that threatened to force their way out of her.

Mitch stopped mid-sentence and glared at his sister.

"Don't you ever let them come back here again," he said, his voice low, menacing.

"But," she stammered, "but they're coming back… the last time… tonight."

"Tonight!" Mitch's shout rattled the plates in the cupboard behind Suzanne's head.

"Yes… yes, tonight. And they… they want us to be there. They've been getting some strange… um, readings… recordings and such. They think it might help if we… if someone who lived in the house… who might be familiar to… to the ghosts… were here."

Mitch stared at her. His mouth opened as if to speak, then shut. He closed his eyes, pinched the bridge of his nose between his finger and thumb, took several deep breaths, and shook his head.

He began to laugh. It was an unnerving sound, and Suzanne shrank further away from him. He pointed his finger at her and shook his head once more, then, to Suzanne's complete surprise, her brother walked right past her, down the hall, and out the front door.

He got into his car, still shaking his head, and drove away.

Suzanne didn't know what to think. For a few moments she stood frozen, grasping the counter behind her. She realized as her lungs suddenly gulped for air that she'd been holding her breath.

When Suzanne got back to her own house, her brother's things were gone. He'd packed up and disappeared; headed back home, she supposed.

Left her here once again to deal with everything, as usual.

Suzanne sighed, looked up the stairs at the door to the larger guest room, still tightly shut, and went into the kitchen to start some tea.

The ghost hunters – the crackpots, Mitch had called them – were going to conduct their last investigation just a few hours later, once the sun had gone down and the house was dark.

They had asked Suzanne, and Mitch too, if he'd agreed, which she'd known he never would, to join them, to provide what they hoped might be a familiar presence to whatever – whoever? – might be haunting the house.

Mitch might think it was crazy, but Mitch was never here, and Suzanne, weak and frightened though she was, suddenly realized she didn't care what Mitch thought.

She was going to the house with the research team that night, and Mitch could go drive off a bridge for all she cared.

CHAPTER SIXTEEN

Mitch, Millie, Suzanne

Mitch

Mitch drove in a general westerly direction.

He didn't know yet if he was going home or not. He had certainly thought about it. He also thought about turning around and diving straight back to Hillview.

For the moment, his mind pinged back and forth between the choices, between thoughts and memories and disbelief.

Several times he shook his head, attempting to clear his thoughts. His sister and her wild theories about ghosts. Mitch chuckled to himself at the thought, but it was uneasy amusement.

In the back of his mind was an annoying itch of an idea, a half-formed thought that he did his best not to finish.

Suzanne's ideas were wild, but wilder still was the feeling worming its way through Mitch's brain: standing in the kitchen, avoiding looking at the basement door, he'd felt, for a brief moment, the unsettling aura of some unseen presence.

But it couldn't have been a ghost. It just couldn't.

He didn't believe in such things.

Millie

Millie was lying at the bottom of the basement stairs. The floor was cold beneath her.

Millie was asleep in her bed, warm and soft.

Millie was standing in the darkened downstairs hallway, listening for something she couldn't name but knew was there.

Millie was falling down the stairs, each bump against each step causing a pain in a different part of her body.

Millie was sitting in her favorite chair in the parlor, watching the snow fall.

Millie was asleep, or awake, or unconscious, or dead.

Millie drifted in darkness.

Suzanne

Somewhere in the back of Suzanne's mind passed the thought that today was the Winter Solstice, the shortest day of the year, and yet the day passed slowly.

She was due to meet with the team at six o'clock in the evening. The hours crept by.

She had a glass of wine, then two, then three, sitting in her living room watching the great red circle of the sun arc across the sky.

From time to time, she would glance beyond the edges of the town, up the hill, to the dark house that sat waiting for her.

She thought once or twice of going up to visit her mother, but the thought was half-hearted, an attempt at being dutiful, no emotion or desire to buoy it up and change thought to action.

She'd told her mother that Mitch would be here today and she'd bring him up to visit, but of course now that wasn't going to happen.

Suzanne didn't really want to spend time with her mother. Each time she went, she sat and talked and cried, but no response from her mother was ever forthcoming. Not that she really expected her to answer. Millie hadn't answered in a long time.

Suzanne waited for evening.

Millie

Millie's vision was still a nighttime darkness, but her ears picked up snatches of sound.

There were voices, distant and distorted. At times they seemed familiar. Once or twice she thought she heard the voices of her children, Suzanne and Mitch, but the black void in which she floated whisked the sounds away beyond reach.

For a time, she seemed to float through the house, vision blurred, the walls like spinning vortices around her, the ground nebulous, her feet floating inches above it as her body drifted.

Her eyes tried to focus through the gray fog that had descended everywhere.

A large rectangular shape sat on the floor in front of her. Momentarily, the fog pulled back and Millie recognized in some far distant part of her mind that it was her husband's toolbox.

Arthur! The cry shot through her, booming loudly in the cavern between her ears.

A voice, a man's voice, called from behind her. She didn't turn but slid backward along the hall like a balloon on a string tugged along by a child. A man's voice. Arthur? Davey? Mitch? A woman crying. Suzanne?

Millie drifted up through the swirling mist and back into blackness.

Mitch

Mitch gripped the steering wheel and cursed under his breath.

This nonsense had to stop.

He wrenched the car around at the first place the road was wide enough and pointed himself back toward the east. He'd been driving aimlessly for five hours, and now another five hours stretched out ahead of him like a dark highway.

A dark highway that led right back to Hillview, to his hysterical sister, to the mother he'd basically abandoned, to the house that sat brooding high on the hill outside of town.

To ghosts?

Mitch wasn't sure. But something seemed to be calling him, pulling him back to his old home, his childhood, to everything he'd tried to run from his whole life.

The road ran on, and the snow began to fall.

CHAPTER SEVENTEEN

Suzanne

The Hillview Paranormal Research Team rented for its official office space a small apartment on the second floor of an old building on Main Street, directly above the barber shop.

Suzanne had been surprised at first learning this, as Gerry's real estate office was only half a block down and across the street.

Yet she had never heard of the HPRT until she saw the flyer. Perhaps things could be kept secret in small towns after all.

Snow was beginning to fall on as Suzanne maneuvered her car into the slanted space outside the barber shop.

She clutched her purse tightly against her stomach as she entered the building and walked up the stairs. Every single step groaned beneath her weight.

At the top of the stairs, a short hallway led to a single door standing half open. A piece of white paper with HILLVIEW PARANOMAL RESEARCH TEAM printed simply on it was taped to the door.

Suzanne knocked lightly. The low hum of voices beyond stopped at the sound. She pushed her way further in, nerves making her stomach do somersaults as she entered.

A tall, brunette woman in her late twenties stood up and smiled. Suzanne remembered her as Teresa, and she seemed to be the leader of the group.

The other members – a chunky dye-job redhead woman, a petite little blonde, barely of drinking age, and a tall Viking of a man with long hair twisted into a knot on the top of his head – nodded politely at her from their seats around the table.

"Suzanne! Come in, come in. Sit down. We have so much to tell you."

Teresa was practically bouncing with excitement as she led Suzanne to an empty seat at the table.

The young man – Jackson, if Suzanne remembered correctly – was messing about with a tangle of wires that seemed to sprout from a laptop on the table in front of him, connecting to headphones and other electronic devices she couldn't begin to name.

Suzanne pulled her coat closer around her and sat down, her back straight and her purse clutched in her lap like a shield.

Teresa's eyes glanced to the door.

"Didn't you say your brother would be coming with you tonight as well?"

Suzanne bit at the inside of her cheek for a moment before she answered. "He decided not to come."

Simple answers were best. No need to air your dirty laundry in front of strangers, like her mother had always said.

A flash of concern wrinkled Teresa's forehead and she looked to the rest of the team. The redhead – Melissa? - shrugged. None of their business, really.

"OK, well we can just go ahead and get started then!"

Teresa's voice was gratingly cheerful. Suzanne flinched away from it.

The younger woman – Carrie, like the Stephen King novel – giggled. Melissa frowned and shot her a look that reminded Suzanne of her mother – stern and disapproving.

Teresa took a deep breath to calm herself. Jackson finished fiddling with the cords and gave her a nod. Everyone was ready.

Everyone except Suzanne.

She wanted to know what they'd found but was scared at the same time.

Scared they'd found some evil spirit living in her mother's house. Scared that was what caused her mother to fall down the stairs. Scared she'd been a horrible daughter for not noticing that something was wrong and protecting her mother. Scared that she'd have to go into the house and deal with things with that evil still there.

Even more scared that they'd found nothing, that her mother, and now even she herself had been seeing, hearing, feeling things that were only in their minds.

Scared that her brother was right, and she really was going crazy.

"Are you alright?" Teresa asked, looking at her intently.

"Oh, oh yes, sorry. I was just… thinking." Suzanne managed to push more confidence into her voice than she actually felt.

"Please, go on."

Teresa gathered up a stack of stapled paper bundles and passed them out, one to each member of the team and one to Suzanne. Suzanne read the cover page:

CASE NOTES
PARANORMAL RESEARCH TEAM
CASE #04
NOVEMBER 16 – DECEMBER 21, 2020
PARTICIPANTS: TERESA RUTLEDGE, JACKSON GREEN, CARRIE JAMESON, MELISSA NEWARK

Teresa explained that they would all be going over the case notes from each investigation date together, as well as reviewing some video and audio recordings, before discussing their plan for that night's investigation.

Around the table, everyone nodded and murmured.

Suzanne's mouth went dry and her right leg, crossed over her left, bounced nervously up and down beneath the table as the team revealed their findings to her.

Each new line of the reports seemed to inject a shot of something bitter and roiling into her stomach.

There had been thumps and bumps, creaks on the stairs, cold spots, manipulation of the thermostat, ghostly music, lights going on and off by themselves, items moved, phantom smells, doors opening on their own, furniture shaking, responsive knocking, shadow figures, and disembodied voices.

Seeing the words on the page and hearing them read off like dry lists of facts was bad enough, but worse was yet to come.

When the pages had been read and Suzanne's head was buzzing with all the new information, Jackson turned the laptop toward her and handed her a pair of big bulky headphones.

"Now we'll show you the evidence we've caught."

The first thing he pulled up was video.

Night vision cameras had picked out the rooms and halls of her mother's house in an unnerving wash of greenish light. A time stamp in the upper right corner told Suzanne that this video was taken at 12:50 a.m., November 30.

She recognized the angle. Someone was standing in the kitchen doorway, pointing their camera down the hall toward the front of the house.

"There!" Jackson pointed to a spot on the screen, "Did you see it?"

Suzanne shook her head. Had there been anything to see?

Jackson backed the video up a few seconds and showed her exactly where to look. She furrowed her eyebrows and leaned in closer to the screen. She supposed that brief shift of darkness along the wall could be a shadow moving, but she felt unconvinced.

Her doubt must have shown on her face because Jackson quickly said, "Just wait! That's only the beginning! There's more!"

A second video showed the disturbing scene of Mitch's childhood bedroom, the bed knocking violently against the wall.

A third video showed the kitchen table moving on its own, a shocked Jackson sitting in the chair next to it and staring, open-mouthed, as it moved.

Another video: a shadowy shape moving across the kitchen as the entire team looked on.

Another: close up shots of a digital thermometer, showing one temperature, then swinging to point in a different direction, the numbers on the display screen dropping rapidly.

Another: A panning shot of the kitchen in utter disarray.

(Melissa: "Any chance you'd been up there, cooking?" Suzanne shook her head, afraid that if she tried to speak no sound would come.)

When the videos stopped and Suzanne thought she had taken all her brain could handle, Jackson's grin grew even wider as he pulled on his own headphones and said,

"Now for the good stuff."

The audio clips were pulled up on the laptop, graphs of spiking lines across the screen.

The first recordings were of various bumps and creaks that could be anything from someone walking to the house settling. Suzanne relaxed a bit.

Then came the unmistakable sound of the stairs creaking. She heard the first creak, held her breath, waiting the amount of time tucked away as memory in her head, and right on target the second creaking stair, further along, sounded as well.

She glanced up at the team. The girls looked expectant; Jackson's eyebrows were raised in excitement.

The next recording featured the voices of the investigators, then silence, filled in by a faint tinny music. Suzanne shivered.

A series of recordings: the team asking questions and expecting knocks for answers. It was hard for Suzanne to tell from the sounds which knocks were made by the team and which were supposedly made by something else, but she could hear the excitement in their recorded voices as what she guessed were supernatural knocks rang back in response.

A recording of what sounded like someone crying. Suzanne felt her own eyes prickle with unexpected tears.

Jackson was practically vibrating with the happiness of his discoveries as he pulled up the next clip.

"Now this," he said, pointing at the spike in center of the graph, "is the big one."

Suzanne wasn't sure she was ready for the big one. She'd been – not frightened exactly, but certainly bothered by the things she'd seen and heard already.

She glanced to Teresa, standing over her. Teresa nodded encouragingly. Suzanne fitted the headphones back over her ears and listened:

Teresa: "We know you're here with us, we can feel you. We are here to help you. Do you want us to help you?"

Silence.

Teresa: "My name is Teresa. These are my friends, Melissa, Carrie, and Jackson. We don't mean you any harm. Can you tell us your name?"

Silence.

Teresa: "We would really love it if you'd communicate with us. Please speak to us. Tell us your name."

Silence.

But not silence.

Suzanne looked questioningly at Jackson.

"What *was* that?" She had heard something – a voice, quiet, distant, a word perhaps, two syllables.

Jackson grinned. "You heard it!"

Suzanne nodded. She'd heard it but she wasn't sure what it was she had heard.

"OK, now, look, we cleaned up the audio a bit, cut out any background noise and *this* is what we got…"

He pulled up a new, smaller clip. Suzanne adjusted the headphones and nodded at him to start it.

The very end of Teresa's last question sounded in her ears. A brief silence, and then the sound. The voice. Suzanne's blood ran cold.

The voice was muted, distorted, but the word was plain enough.

"Did you hear it?" Teresa asked. Suzanne nodded. She felt frozen in place.

"Here, let me put that on a loop for you," Jackson offered.

Suzanne really didn't want him to, didn't want to hear the voice, the word again, but she couldn't move, couldn't speak.

The voice came through the wires again and again, over and over. Fear spiked through her, her heartbeat pounded, thrumming in her ears and echoing back inside the headphones.

Her vision clouded, black at the edges, and the room swam in circles in front of her.

"Oh my God, she's gonna pass out!" Melissa cried out suddenly, and the last thing Suzanne saw as the world tilted and she slid sideways in her chair was Teresa's worried face as her arms reached to catch her.

The last thing she heard was the name repeated over and over in her ears: *Arthur…Arthur…Arthur.*

The last thing she thought as her body hit the floor: *Daddy?*

CHAPTER EIGHTEEN

Mitch

Mitch's eyes were heavy.

He drove with his window down and the radio blaring classic rock, the volume turned up as high as it would go.

The snow was coming fast and thick now, the windshield wipers swaying back and forth with a lulling regularity as they wiped the front window clean of the falling flakes over and over again.

The world was taking on the hues and shape of a winter wonderland. He'd have thought it was beautiful, if he wasn't so intent on getting back to Hillview before it got worse.

He wasn't worried about the snow, really, he'd driven in it plenty of times, especially when he'd lived out east for a few years when he was younger.

What was worrying him, however, was how difficult it was becoming to keep his eyes open, with forty-five minutes of driving still ahead of him. He slapped himself across the face a few times and took another drink of the now-cold coffee he'd purchased at the last gas station twenty miles back.

There was not another stop between here and Hillview, not a gas station or a house or anything else, just a long, dark stretch of road that curved through the mountains, through the snow.

He drove on.

Millie

It was snowing.

Millie could see it outside her window. She smiled. She thought of Christmas trees and gingerbread, snowmen and carols.

Tucked warmly beneath her blankets, she sang the old Christmas songs to herself. Many of the words were forgotten now, but she hummed through the places she couldn't remember.

She thought of the four of them, she and Arthur and the kids, sitting around the piano downstairs in the parlor, she herself playing a simple accompaniment as the others sang along.

Smiles and laughter and voices not entirely in tune, but happy, nonetheless.

Where were the kids?

Suzanne should certainly be up to visit any moment now, and still she swore she had heard Mitch's voice earlier.

Perhaps they were planning a Christmas surprise. That would be nice.

Millie gazed at the snow, and her eyelids grew heavy. A lovely sort of blankness seeped into her mind, and she slept.

Suzanne

Suzanne came groggily back to consciousness.

She could hear voices, quiet, concerned, above her. Her head ached fiercely. Her body felt jittery, like she'd had an abundance of caffeine, or a vein full of cocaine. And something was shoving uncomfortably into her shoulder.

She opened her eyes a crack. Dark shapes loomed over her. Her equilibrium seemed to balance out gradually. She was horizontal, she knew that much.

She raised her hand to shield her eyes from the bright lights overhead. The shapes above her resolved into people. Teresa, Melissa, Carrie, gathered tightly around her. Jackson's head and shoulders rising above and just behind the others.

Suzanne looked at herself. She was stretched ungracefully on an old couch in the corner of the room,

135

her head and shoulders propped up against the hard wood of the armrest.

She sat up carefully, and the women around her rushed to steady her.

Their voices were a babbling, cackling henhouse of concern, the words tangling up together in her brain. Suzanne held one hand to her aching head and the other out in front of her in a silencing motion.

"What happened? Did I… faint?"

She had never fainted in her life, but if she was going to imagine the way fainting felt, this would certainly be it.

She hoped she hadn't done anything embarrassing. More embarrassing than the fainting itself, anyway.

She *had* fainted, Teresa explained. They had moved her here to the couch, and she'd been out cold for about five minutes.

Well, that wasn't *too* dramatic, Suzanne thought wryly.

Then the memory of why she had fainted slammed into her thoughts. The sound, the voice, the word, the name. She looked up at the team.

"That voice….it said 'Arthur'. That's my father."

The team looked at one another before turning back to her and nodding.

"Do you think… is my father haunting the old house?"

Suzanne found it hard to believe. Why would he? And why only now? He'd been dead for twenty-seven years.

The team wasn't sure.

It could be him. It was certainly a compelling piece of evidence. They might find out more during tonight's investigation, if Suzanne was still up for it.

She was a little wobbly on her feet, a little frightened, but she was ready. Or at least she was going to pretend to be. Fear mixed with unease and excitement inside of her. She was curious about and yet dreading what they might find.

But she was definitely going.

Mitch

The driving was slow.

Freezing rain had begun to fall along with the snow, and in places the road was already glazing over with ice.

Mitch's car crept along, his headlights barely showing him the few feet of road directly in front of him. The road curved through the foothills of the Ozark Mountains. There were no helpful streetlights; no truck would be coming along dumping sand on these lanes to make the ice less treacherous.

Mitch leaned forward over the steering wheel, gripping it tightly with both hands, squinting into the whiteness beyond.

If he had been less intent on the road ahead of him, if his music hadn't been turned up quite so loud, he might have noticed the truck that came rattling, too wild, too fast, along the road behind him.

As it was, he was surprised completely when the front of the truck met the back of his car on the icy road, utterly shocked as his car spun across the asphalt as the truck pushed it sideways, appalled at the driver's carelessness as the truck zoomed on past without even stopping.

Most unexpected of all, though, was the moment when his car tipped off the edge of the road and plunged a short distance down the hill beyond, with an echoing crunch as it crashed head-on into a huge oak tree.

Mitch felt strangely free of pain as he climbed out of the car, and in the back of his doctor's mind he rehearsed the fact that a relaxed body is less likely to suffer injury that a tense one, and he supposed he should then be thankful that he hadn't seen the truck coming, hadn't had time to brace for impact before the world spun in a circle around him.

Pain free, yes, but not frustration free.

There was no way he was getting that car back up onto the road by himself. It would take a tow truck and a winch for that, and looking at the front of his car, the hood caved in around the sturdy tree trunk, smoke escaping from the misused engine, he doubted the car would still run even if he could get it back up.

He would have to call Suzanne, have her come pick him up.

He knew that he was only a few miles outside of town now. It wouldn't take long. He knew he'd be okay in the ten minutes it might take her to drive up and find him.

He reached in his pocket for his cell phone. It wasn't there. Mitch's face darkened. He always kept it in his front left pocket.

He checked the other pockets just to be sure. Nothing. Had it fallen out in the car somewhere? He eyed the slippery slope he'd just climbed up. He started toward it when a thought struck him.

He could see himself at the gas station he'd stopped at a couple of hours ago, could see himself using the restroom, taking out his phone to check the time and how many miles remained, setting it down on the edge of the sink as he washed his hands, walking out to buy his coffee.

With a sudden certain dread he knew he'd left his phone sitting in that dingy little gas station bathroom.

Walking into town it must be, then.

He turned up the collar of his coat, tucked his hands into his pockets, and started along the road in the darkness.

CHAPTER NINETEEN

Suzanne

Suzanne didn't quite trust herself to drive.

Instead, the whole team rode together in the large van: Teresa driving, Suzanne given the place of honor in the passenger seat, Melissa, Carrie, and Jackson squeezed together in the middle row, and the entire back of the van filled with large, black, hard-plastic cases.

Suzanne assumed the boxes held all of the team's equipment.

No one spoke much as they made the short drive along Main Street, out beyond the edge of the town proper, and up the road to the old house.

The team was filled with excitement. Suzanne was filled with apprehension, and a touch of fear. Along with the fear, however, ran a tiny current of exhilaration, sparking through her like an old forgotten remnant of her younger days.

This felt just a little bit dangerous.

Once upon a time, she'd liked a bit of danger. She snorted a breath out her nose, a laugh held captive behind her closed lips.

Yes, a bit of danger might be just what she needed.

It felt strange to stand back as someone else unlocked the door to her mother's house, stranger still to watch a parade of young people march back and forth from the van to the kitchen with the equipment cases, like they knew the house as well as she did, like perhaps they were the ones who had lived here, and she was simply a stranger watching this curious spectacle.

The team's steps left footprints in the gathering snow as Suzanne gazed up into the evening sky, watching the snowflakes fall.

She shivered once, pulled her coat closer around her, and went inside.

Suzanne roamed a bit while the team set up their equipment.

The house, never changing, sat static in just the way it had been since she was a child. There was, of course, a thick layer of dust beginning to accumulate on all the once-shining surfaces, and a stale sort of odor hung in the air, but other than that, everything was exactly the same.

Each piece of furniture sat in the exact place it had sat for fifty years.

Each book in the small office stood in its same place on the shelf.

Suzanne knew where each can of beans or box of rice would be in the kitchen cabinets, each dish stacked in precise order, each and every silly little tchotchke on every sideboard, table, and shelf.

"Just another ten minutes or so, Suzanne," Teresa called, sticking her head around the corner, a coil of cords in her hands.

Suzanne nodded. She stopped at the bottom of the stairs, hand on the banister. The second floor was nothing but a hazy darkness above her. She started forward, one foot in front of the other, up the creaking steps.

The second-floor hallway had six doors. To Suzanne's left were the doors to her parents' room, and further on, the door which was always locked when she was a child, but she knew now to have been her Uncle Davey's room.

Her mother hadn't liked to talk about him, his death an aching loss in her soul that seemed to have never gone away.

To the right were three more bedrooms: first Mitch's, then Suzanne's old room, then the spare that had been used for storage.

At the very end of the hall stood the door to the one bathroom they'd all shared.

Gerry had been appalled at that. *Really, a big, huge house with only one full bathroom upstairs and one half bath downstairs?*

She supposed it wasn't the modern way of doing things, but Suzanne had never minded only the one bathroom to share. But Gerry thought in square footage and dollar signs, so he looked at things differently than she did.

Suzanne pulled out her phone and turned on its flashlight.

She made her way to the second door on the right: her old bedroom. The door gave a quiet creak as she pushed it open.

She flipped on the light.

This room held an even stronger feeling of disuse than the rest of the house, and yet it was also the room that had seen the most changes.

The downstairs rooms were the same as ever. Suzanne knew that her mother's bedroom was the same, knew that Mitch's old room had been preserved exactly as he left it when he went off to college all those years ago.

And Uncle Davey's room, of course, hadn't been changed in seventy-five years.

But this room, her room, though still several decades past its last renovation, had at least been changed a little.

Mitch's room might be a shrine to his childhood, left behind neatly and without regret all those years ago, but Suzanne was the one who had come back home.

In shame and despair she had returned to her mother's house all those years ago, and though she'd only lived there for a few months, she'd done her best to update her old bedroom while she was there.

There were no toys here, no school awards, even the posters that had decorated her teenage walls were gone. The room was plain, stark, depressing.

Suzanne sat on the old bed, a little puff of dust rising around her. Her hands spread the top quilt smooth.

She'd been so determined, when she came back here after the California fiasco, to grow up, to leave behind all the wild childish dreams that had led her out west to begin with.

She sighed into the dim emptiness, a sigh which held thirty years of loneliness, dissatisfaction, and frustration. The room seemed to sigh back at her, a shifting in the cool air around her. Suzanne's skin pricked up in goosebumps as tears stung her eyes.

She hated this room.

She got up and walked firmly, decisively out into the hallway, closing the door behind her.

She could hear the quiet murmur of the team's voices downstairs, and she followed the sound to the kitchen.

Mitch

The snow wasn't letting up.

Mitch's progress was slow, his legs weighted down by cold and exhaustion.

The woods on either side of the road were dark and silent; the whole world was so quiet that he could hear the fall of the snow, the impact of a thousand tiny ice crystals striking the trees, the road, his shoulders.

He knew the town was close. If not for the snow, he felt sure he'd be able to see the lights of people's houses, the Christmas strands strung across Main Street.

He was close, surely he was. He just had to keep walking.

CHAPTER TWENTY

Millie

Millie woke once more in the darkness.

She swung sideways on the bed and stood up.

Her legs felt weak, and she waited a few moments for her muscles to wake up. She shuffled to the door, opened it, and looked out.

The house was quiet, and almost completely dark. It seemed strange to her that no one would be home at this hour.

She went down the hallway and stopped outside the door to Suzanne's room, where the sole light in the entire house shone out through a crack in the door.

She stepped into the room and looked around. Suzanne wasn't there. The room was plain, bare, boring, as Suzanne's entire life had been since she returned from California all those years ago.

Millie's heart ached suddenly with the pain of her child. Poor Suzanne. So full of wild hope and dreams when she was young, so full of sadness and despair now.

Millie's long-dormant maternal love seemed to rush up inside her and a tear slipped down her cheek. She'd been so disappointed in Suzanne, and it had driven a wedge between them ever since.

Millie felt dizzy with it, and for a brief disorienting moment the room seemed to spin up like a house caught in a tornado, a rush of sighing wind circling round the room as Millie stood in its center.

Just as quickly, the feeling stopped. Millie let out a long, grieving sigh of her own.

Oh, *Suzanne*, she thought, *my poor little girl.*

Suzanne

"OK," Teresa said, "We're all set up. Are you ready?"

Suzanne looked nervously over the piles of equipment and nodded. Inside she felt half numb, like this must all be a dream; she couldn't possibly really be standing in her mother's house with a team of ghost hunters, hoping and fearing coming face to face with the spirit of her father.

It was crazy, really, crazy to think about and even crazier to do, yet here she was.

Teresa watched her closely, and the rest of the team watched Teresa.

The team leader looked uncertain for a moment, wondering if taking a possibly emotionally unstable woman who had just recovered from an extreme reaction to a piece of evidence on an investigation was really the smartest thing to do.

But Suzanne lifted her chin and looked her straight in the eyes, determined, so Teresa nodded once and grabbed a handheld camera.

She gave it to Suzanne and gave her a quick explanation of how to turn it on and off, how she should use the lighted screen only as a guide and make sure to look up from it regularly, lest it skew her balance in the darkness.

Suzanne followed the girls as they made their way slowly down the hall. Teresa stopped for a moment to point her camera at the thermostat.

"Sixty-five degrees," she noted.

They crept carefully up the stairs. For a moment the creaking of the staircase seemed like it would go on endlessly as four pairs of feet hit the offending steps one after the other.

Suzanne brought up the rear, holding lightly to the banister and trying to ignore the vertigo that made her head swim.

At the top of the stairs, the group paused, clustered together in the small area. Through the green light of her display screen, Suzanne watched Teresa turn toward her.

"Suzanne," Teresa whispered, "Did you turn a light on up here?"

Suzanne looked in the direction that Teresa's finger was pointing. Halfway down the hall a sickly yellow strip of light showed underneath her old bedroom door.

"Oh," Suzanne said, "Yes. Sorry."

She couldn't believe she'd left the light on.

If her mother had been here to see her wasting electricity, she'd have given her a lecture.

Suzanne clamped her hand over her mouth as a wild giggle threatened to escape. Up ahead, the strip of light bloomed into a triangular glow across the floorboards and then disappeared as Teresa reached inside the door and flipped the switch.

Suzanne blushed with embarrassment and was thankful that no one could see her reddened cheeks in the darkness.

A whisper cut through the quiet: "Let's start in here."

Suzanne couldn't tell who was speaking, but as one the group moved to the left, into her mother's bedroom, and she followed.

A silhouette – Melissa, by the vague shape of it – walked around the room pointing a small device at all the walls and furniture.

"She's taking temperature recordings," spoke a soft voice next to Suzanne, and she jerked away from the unexpected sound.

"Sorry, sorry."

It was Carrie standing next to her, a concerned hand on Suzanne's arm.

"Didn't mean to frighten you."

Suzanne nodded her understanding, then realized Carrie might not be able to see her in the darkness.

"It's OK," she whispered.

Melissa had finished her circuit of the room and came back to the group standing just inside the door.

"Nothing out of the ordinary. Pretty consistent all around."

Mitch

Mitch had stopped thinking.

Stopped thinking about the distance to the town, the grade of the road, the amount of snow coating his hair and shoulders and seeping in through the hems of his pants.

Only one word pounded through his brain with the focus borne of life-or-death necessity: *go go go go.*

Blindly, he put one frozen foot in front of the other. Only vaguely did he register the lights that surrounded him, blurred into starry shimmering glows by the snowfall, as he walked down Main Street.

No one was in the darkened shops; everyone was at home, safe and warm. No cars passed the lone man who walked, shivering and half-frozen in the middle of the road.

Go… go… go.

The words repeated in his head, and the last cognizant shred of consciousness within him slowly altered the words as he trudged on.

Home… home… home.

Suzanne

A tiny glowing red light appeared in Teresa's hand.

"This is a digital audio recorder," she explained to Suzanne, who could just make out a small rectangular shape around the light.

Teresa moved forward and the light settled as she sat it on the bed.

"Come on, let's try an EVP session."

The women sat on the floor in a half circle around the bed.

"Now," Teresa said, leaning close to Suzanne and speaking quietly, "We'll start with the standard questions, and then you talk. See if you can get anyone – your father or anyone else – to come through and talk to a familiar person, OK?"

Suzanne nodded, caught herself again, and whispered, "OK."

Teresa pushed a button on the recorder, then settled back onto the floor and spoke,

"EVP session, Carver house, December 21, 2020, 8:55 pm, master bedroom, Teresa, Melissa, Carrie, and Suzanne Carver-Bowles present."

She waited a few moments, all quiet in the room except for the faint movement of clothing as the women got comfortable on the floor, then she spoke again, louder and clearly.

"My name is Teresa, and I am here with my friends. We mean you no harm. We wish to speak with any spirits who live in this house. Is there anyone there?

Silence.

"Can you tell us your name?"

Suzanne strained her ears but heard nothing.

"Why are you here, in this house? Is the house important to you?"

Still nothing.

"We have another friend here with us tonight. Her name is Suzanne. She grew up in this house. Do you know her? Would you like to speak with Suzanne?"

No sounds stirred the air.

Teresa laid a hand gently on Suzanne's knee encouragingly. Suzanne took a deep breath, swallowed hard.

She didn't really know what to say; she felt silly talking into the darkness to someone – some-thing? – that might not really even be there.

She started out cautiously.

"Um, hello? It's Suzanne. Suzanne Carver? Do… do you know me? Do you remember me? Would you like to talk to me?"

They waited, four women sitting in the bedroom floor like little girls playing at some strange forbidden game, and they listened.

The silence seemed to wrap around Suzanne's body, reaching dark tendrils into her ears and drumming against her eardrums in time with her heartbeat.

"Again," Teresa whispered next to her.

Suzanne wiggled a bit, her back already growing stiff from sitting on the hard floor in a cold house. She cleared her throat a little to buy herself time to think.

"Hello, Suzanne again. Still. Can you say something to me?"

She paused, trembling as she took in a shallow breath.

"Daddy? Daddy are you here? Is it you, Daddy? Do you want to talk to me?"

Perhaps five beats of silence passed before the door behind them creaked.

A wash of goosebumps started on Suzanne's shoulders and rushed outward, up her neck and over her scalp, down her midsection and across her thighs at the same time.

She tensed, curling into herself against the feeling, and gasped as a shroud of icy air settled around her. Her bones vibrated inside her as wave after wave of cold poured over her body.

The other women scuttled backward away from her on the floor as Suzanne sat rigid, unable to move. Teresa had her camera trained on Suzanne's figure, the older woman's eyes huge and frightened on the green display screen.

Melissa pointed her thermometer at Suzanne.

"Drastic temperature change! Sixty-one degrees and dropping!"

Carrie had crawled backward all the way across the room and was sitting, back against the wall, staring, her camera forgotten in her hands.

"Suzanne?" Teresa asked cautiously, "Are you alright?"

Suzanne didn't speak, didn't move, but her eyes darted toward Teresa. She wasn't alright. She wasn't hurt but she was so cold; her limbs felt like heavy weights, weights shot through with icy pain, and fingers of darkness stretched across her vision.

The now familiar feeling of faintness swept across her, the world closing in to a small pinprick of red light on the bed, her heartbeat drumming loudly in her ears, nausea rising in her stomach, until –

Everything stopped.

Mitch

Mitch could see the house ahead.

He only had to reach it. *Go… home… go… home.*

He could barely feel his feet as they pushed through the snow. He could barely feel his arm as it reached to knock on the front door. His hand stretching out in front of him looked alien to him, like someone else's body in action. His palm flopped flat against the wood of the door, and to his surprise, the door creaked open.

Unlocked? He could barely believe it. By what freak chance of luck was this?

The house looked dark, deserted, but the front door was unlocked, the catch not even properly latched. He leaned his weight against the door until it opened enough to admit him.

Warmth rushed over him as he stumbled inside and collapsed in the nearest chair he could find.

Suzanne

Suzanne slumped over on the floor, fully conscious still but unable to hold herself up now that the paralyzing cold was gone.

Teresa and Melissa rushed toward her at the same moment a crackle of static came over their walkie-talkies.

Jackson's voice cut through, quiet and urgent.

"Uh, guys? The front door just opened by itself."

For a moment the four women looked at each other, eyes wide, bodies framed in odd positions as they froze mid-movement.

Suzanne pushed herself up onto her elbows and tried to make herself breathe calmly, in and out, in and out, as her heart pounded away like a maddened drum inside her chest.

Teresa and Melissa each grasped one of her arms and helped her to her feet. The room tilted for a few seconds, first one way and then the other, before settling back into a relative steadiness.

Millie

When she returned to her own bedroom, Millie felt immediately that something was off.

She knew the house was empty and yet she felt that it was not. She paused on the way to her bed, standing perfectly still in the middle of her room. A rush of heat started at her feet and flamed up her legs. She tried to ignore it as she listened.

Did she hear footsteps on the walk, on the porch? Was someone coming home?

She heard the quiet creak of the front door. Footsteps. Her first thought was that Suzanne had come home, but even in her old and addled brain she registered that the footsteps didn't sound like a woman.

They sounded like a man, heavy and slow.

She remembered hearing Mitch's voice earlier, like a dream, and her heart barely dared to hope it: Mitch had come home.

Suzanne

"I'm OK, I'm OK," Suzanne whispered, as much to herself as to the women standing on either side of her.

Carrie still sat on the floor, her head now turned, looking out into the darkness of the hallway and down the stairs.

Teresa made sure Suzanne was steady on her feet and then went to help Carrie up.

"Come on, quietly, slowly, downstairs. Let's check out that door."

Suzanne followed Teresa, with Carrie and Melissa close behind. Her head was beginning to hurt, a slight but steady pain at the base of her skull that pulsed in time with her heartbeat. She did her best to ignore it.

It was easy to see that the front door was indeed open. The snow had accumulated rapidly outside, and even the dim bit of moonlight that fought its way down through the falling flakes reflected back off the snowy ground with an unmistakable brightness.

Through the half-open door this light shone into the house and lit the hall in an unearthly glow.

Suzanne sat on the bottom stair, leaning against the stair rail, as the others examined the door. Was it possible the door had been left unlocked, slightly ajar? Had a gust of wind perhaps pushed it open?

For several minutes they tried to find any natural cause for the opening. They closed the door all the way and Teresa pushed against it from the outside. It didn't budge.

They closed it most of the way but without latching and Teresa pushed again. The door opened slightly. They repeated this experiment but waited to see if the strength of the wind would push the door open. Nothing happened.

Outside, the bare tree branches groaned in the wind, but the breeze that moved them was not enough to push the door open.

Teresa disappeared down the hall for a few moments and returned with a camera on a tripod. She set it up in a corner, pointed at the front door, and turned it on.

"That's all we can do for now," she said. "If it happens again, hopefully the camera will catch something that can help explain it."

"OK, now," Teresa went on, "I think we should try the knocking experiment again. We often get a response from that, and I'd like Suzanne to experience it, and see if we can get even more interaction with her here. Ok, Suzanne?"

Suzanne didn't answer.

The other women turned to look at her. In the darkness she was a little more than a formless shape at the bottom of the stairs.

Melissa, standing nearest her, reached out and gently laid her hand on Suzanne's shoulder. She shook her, lightly and carefully.

"Suzanne?"

Suzanne slowly reached up and placed her own hand over Melissa's, patting it slowly like a mother consoling an upset child. Still she did not speak. She couldn't.

While the other women had been occupied with the door, Suzanne had been gazing about her in the half-light when something caught her eye.

A pale light, like the glow emitted from a tiny fire, bluish-white and no bigger than her fist, had been moving slowly about in the parlor just across the hall. Another wave of goosebumps had broken out over her skin, and for some reason her eyes had filled with tears.

She pointed, now, into the parlor, the beam of moonlight coming through the small window in the front door falling on her arm and lighting up her pointing finger so that she seemed half ghostly herself.

The others followed the direction of her outstretched hand and looked into the parlor. Carried gasped. Teresa slowly raised her arm, pointing her camera at the orb which floated near the fireplace.

"Holy crap," Carrie whispered as Teresa took a few cautious steps toward the parlor door.

The light seemed to pulse brighter for a moment, then it suddenly flew downward toward the floor and winked out like a snuffed candle.

Carrie let out a small squeal of a scream and clapped her hand over her mouth.

Teresa turned back to the others, the arm holding her camera shaking.

"You guys," she whispered, "You guys… whoa."

The others nodded solemnly, and as Suzanne's head dropped the tears that had pooled along her lower eyelids broke free and trickled down her cheeks.

The spell broken, she raised her hand and wiped the tears away, warm wetness on her fingertips.

For a minute or two, they all simply stood and let their brains try to process what they had just seen.

"That was totally an orb," Melissa said, wonder and a small amount of disbelief in her voice.

"It was," Teresa agreed.

"And that was definitely no insect or speck of dust. And I got it on camera!"

She grinned.

Everyone smiled, except for Suzanne. She didn't know why precisely, couldn't explain it in words, but she felt enveloped in a horribly dark sadness and despair.

The tears wouldn't stop, falling silently down her cheeks and dropping onto the sleeves of her sweater.

Mitch

He must have passed out for a bit.

When Mitch came to, he was still cold but considerably warmer than he'd been outside in the snow. He waited until the room came into focus around him. All was dark.

The house was mostly quiet, except for a few faint rustlings in the next room that he figured must be mice, having a grand time of it in the spaces between the walls.

He stood, testing his legs to make sure they were steady before he stepped away from the safety of his chair.

Something seemed strange, though he couldn't put his finger on quite what it was. The room seemed familiar and yet wrong. He stood and walked back and forth in the darkness, studying the furniture and walls.

As his mind became more fully awake, it clicked into place. He knew where he was, but it wasn't where he'd intended to be.

He'd meant to walk to Suzanne's house.

Instead, his frozen mind had directed his feet *home*. To his mother's house.

He suddenly felt lightheaded again, and he grabbed the parlor mantel to keep from falling.

His fingers couldn't grasp it, slipping off as his arms reached out, and his whole body crumpled to the floor in a dead faint.

Suzanne

"Oh," Carrie said softly.

Closest to Suzanne, she was the only one to hear the older woman's quiet sniffling.

"Oh, Suzanne. Guys, she's crying."

Suzanne was guided from her spot on the stairs back to the kitchen, where the light of Jackson's monitors made the room glow green.

She was sat gently in a chair at the table and a bottle of water was pressed into her hands. Absentmindedly, she lifted the bottle to her lips and drank. Her eyes stared off into some distant place the others could not see.

"I'm worried about her, you guys," Melissa spoke.

Carrie bit her nails and Teresa frowned.

Suddenly Suzanne's body jerked and the water she'd been drinking came spluttering back from her mouth. She bent forward, coughing violently, choking on the water. Melissa thumped her a few times, hard, on the back.

When Suzanne sat back up, she wiped her mouth with the back of her hand and gave a few more small coughs. Her eyes seemed clearer now, her mind back in the room with them.

She told them all that she was okay, and she tried to explain the feeling that had washed over her back on the stairs, the overwhelming feeling of sadness, hopelessness, loneliness, despair.

She had felt herself falling into it, the emotion a deep, dark, unending well that she tipped into headfirst. She was frustrated at her inability to find the words to truly say what she felt, but the others listened and nodded sympathetically and once she'd finished, she felt a tiny bit better.

"I'm really not sure it's good for you to be here, Suzanne," Teresa said, sitting down across the table from her.

"This all seems to be affecting you quite severely. Maybe we should call it quits for the night and take you home."

"No!" Suzanne spoke the word forcefully.

"No." This time more calmly.

"I don't want to stop. It's just… it's a little much, but I'll be okay. Please."

Teresa looked at Suzanne's pleading face, then glanced around at the others. Their expressions only reflected back her own uncertainty.

"Alright," she agreed.

"But you must promise to tell us as soon as you start to feel anything, OK? I'm really worried about you."

The team gathered once more in the front parlor.

The moon, so bright just a little while before, had been completely obscured by thick white clouds full of snow.

The house felt cocooned, held softly but tightly away from the rest of the world. To the members of the team it felt ominous. To Suzanne it felt strangely comforting.

The women ranged themselves around the room, Teresa and Carrie taking up spots on the floor to either side of the doorway, Suzanne sitting in her mother's old chair, Melissa standing directly behind her with her back to the window.

Teresa pulled out the digital recorder once more, it's red pinprick of light seeming to float in the darkness in the center of the floor. Melissa held her camera at the ready, and Teresa began to speak.

"Hello, to any spirits who may be here with us. We mean you no harm. We wish only to communicate with you. If speaking is too hard, we're going to try knocking again, like this."

Knock, knock! Teresa's knuckles rapped against the floor. Knock, knock!

"Can you make a noise like that for us, please? Can you knock on the floor, or the wall, or bang on something, to let us know you're here?"

They waited and listened.

Teresa lifted her eyes and silently begged whatever presence was there to please make an appearance and not make them look like fools in front of Suzanne.

Thump.

The sound came up through the floorboards. Teresa and Carrie could feel it most, sitting on the floor, but even Suzanne and Melissa felt the vibration in their feet. Suzanne took in a quick breath and raised her hand to her throat.

"OK, that was good, we heard you. Can you do it again, please?"

A moment of silence, then: *thump, thump!*

Teresa was excited. She glanced at Suzanne who now had her hands cupped over her mouth, her eyes huge and round, white in the darkness.

"Can you use those noises to talk to us, please? We will ask you questions, and you can answer by knocking. One knock means yes, and two knocks mean no. Do you understand that?"

There was no hesitation this time: *THUMP!*

Melissa let out a small shriek and pointed toward the fireplace, to where she was watching through the screen of her camera.

A few of the knickknacks on the mantel shook slightly, as though the mantel had been bumped.

The women watched in silence as the figures wobbled a few more times and then stilled.

Millie

As she made her way slowly down the stairs, clutching the railing for support, Millie heard the sound again.

Knock, knock.

She froze on the spot, grip tightening, and held her breath. It came again.

Knock, knock.

As quietly as she could, taking care to step cautiously and lightly on the creaking steps, she made her way down the last few stairs.

Was it Mitch? But why would he be knocking like that?

Millie was frightened and confused. Her own house looked strange to her, like it wasn't her house at all, like it belonged to someone else, and she was the trespasser.

But she could feel the stairs solid beneath her feet and the banister steady in her hands. She was at home, wasn't she?

This was her house, wasn't it?

Mitch

Mitch woke up in the darkness.

He was lying on a hard floor. His head was pounding; his brain felt disconnected.

He realized it felt rather like having a hangover, not that he'd had one of those in years. In front of him on the floor, a short distance away, there was a red light.

A tiny red light, with a bright little corona around it, like looking at a streetlight through a raindrop. The light was steady. Mitch focused on it.

The light made him feel huge and ungainly next to its miniscule presence. And yet it was the only thing he could see, the only point of focus in a world of floating nothingness.

He was focusing rather intently on this small light, willing himself to float closer to it, when a loud noise vibrated up from beneath him.

Knock, knock!

He stiffened. A feeling he had not felt in years, decades, a feeling he had trained himself not to feel – the feeling of fear, of unknowing – spilled slowly through his sluggish veins.

He carefully raised himself up on one elbow, wincing at the sound at his joint met the old threadbare carpet. The red light continued to shine steadily.

Knock, knock!

The sound came again. With a speed he didn't know his middle-aged body still possessed, Mitch pushed up off the floor, thumping ungracefully against the floorboards and banging his shoulder, hard, against some projecting bit of wood or stone as he rose to standing.

Beside him something rattled and shook. He didn't dare turn his head to look.

The red light was below him now; by casting his eyes downward he could see it, grown even smaller from this perspective.

Raising his eyes from the floor, Mitch could make out dark shapes around him. He couldn't be sure what they were – boulders, furniture, people, something – but a creeping dread made him somehow certain that he was not alone here.

Farther on, through an opening between two of the dark shapes, a new light caught his attention.

The light was pale and glowing, and it was moving. It seemed to float down from somewhere above, then pause a moment. He had the feeling that the light, whatever it was, was looking straight at him. It moved toward him, just a little, stopping short of the dark figures standing between them.

It seemed…Mitch could hardly believe what he was seeing, but it seemed as if the light stretched arms out toward him, beckoning.

Stranger still, Mitch felt a strong compulsion to move toward it.

Suzanne

Suzanne and all the other women watched, speechless, as the orb they had seen earlier reappeared near the mantel, gathering the tiny bits of light in the room to it until it retained its previous size.

It hovered motionless for the space of one minute, perhaps two, and then it began to move. Suzanne's eyes followed it as it floated slowly across the room, toward the door.

Sitting in the chair, turning her head slightly as she watched the orb's progress, Suzanne was the first to see beyond the doorway, into the hallway beyond. She gasped and held her hands to her chest. The others turned slowly. Carrie let out a shriek and backed away from the doorway. Teresa and Melissa simply stared.

There, in the hallway beyond the door, was another light. A larger light, hovering closer to the ground, but pulsing softly with a stronger glow that the small orb.

The orb seemed to be floating toward it.

As the two lights met, they both glowed brighter, and the women all threw their hands over their faces to shield their eyes from the blinding light.

Down the hall, in the kitchen, Jackson's chair scraped backward loudly on the wooden floor as the light shone out from the computer monitor where he'd been watching the feed from the hallway camera.

Millie

This surely was her house. It seemed to spin around her, making it hard to breathe, but she knew she was in her own home.

She was on the stairs, at the bottom was the entry hall, just across from that was the parlor. She could see the doorway in the dim light from the kitchen.

She could also see someone moving within.

She crept closer.

It was a person, a silhouette against the wall, a man. *Mitch!*

Her slippered feet took one shambling step toward him, then two, and then she stopped.

She could see, just inside the doorway, two shadowy, indistinct shapes. They flanked the entry like gargoyles, crouching, waiting. She was frightened of them.

They reminded her of something, some other moment, some other night afraid here in her own house; they reminded her of falling, and of pain, and of nothingness. She didn't dare go near them.

Yet beyond them, the shape of Mitch.

She was sure it was him. He seemed to brighten just a little in the darkness, a flash in the eyes that told her she was right, this was Mitch, her Mitch, her little boy come home.

She was suddenly frightened for him, trapped in the room with those shadowy figures. She reached her arms out, imploring him to come out, to come to her.

The shape that was Mitch stepped toward her.

Suzanne

The light lingered a moment and was gone.

The four women took in deep breaths and did their best to remain calm. Melissa held her camera steady, focused beyond the doorway.

Teresa crawled across the floor to Suzanne, resting a hand on her knee.

"Are you OK?" she asked.

Suzanne gulped and whispered that she was.

"I know that was quite a shock to you. It was to all of us."

Here Teresa let out a strange giggle.

"But I think, if you're up for it, we should try an EVP, while the action seems so high and hot."

Suzanne nodded.

Teresa caught the subtle movement against the crack of light now shining through the drapes. She nodded her own head in agreement.

"You can stay sitting right here if you like, Suzanne. We're going to be just out there, near the stairs."

Carrie climbed reluctantly to her feet and joined her fellow team members in the entry way. Melissa held her camera at the ready. Teresa picked up the EVP recorder and started a new session.

Suzanne listened as Teresa called out to the spirits once again.

She was exhausted. Tears threatened to drop from her eyes.

Her head spun with all the impossible experiences she'd just been through. She wanted nothing more than to sleep. She wanted this to be over. She was a little annoyed when Teresa asked her to speak again, but she spoke anyway.

"Hello? Is anyone there? It's me again, Suzanne. Can you please come and talk to us? Please, show me you're here."

They waited in silence for the recorder to pick up a response, and in the quiet a new sound was heard: the crunching of tires on snow.

Suzanne turned and pulled back the drapes. A pair of headlights were making their way slowly up the snowy incline to the house.

The idea that the whole world still existed beyond the darkened rooms of this house seemed unreal for a moment. Who would be coming to the house, and at this time of night?

For a fleeting moment, Suzanne thought that perhaps Mitch had returned after all, but as the lights drew closer, Suzanne recognized not Mitch's small little car, but her husband's truck.

Gerry? Why on earth would he be here?

Suzanne rose and walked on shaky legs to the front door.

"It's my husband," she explained to the others as she opened it.

Gerry was already running as quickly as he could up the slippery sidewalk. "Suzanne!" he shouted. "Oh, Suzanne, thank God!"

Gerry entered the house, brushing snow from his shoulders, and wrapped his wife in his arms.

"Oh, Suzanne, I... I'm so sorry."

Suzanne pulled away from him, confused, looking questioningly into his face.

"Gerry, what? What on earth are you talking about?"

Gerry looked around at the other women. They looked just as confused as Suzanne.

"Why didn't you answer your phone, Suzanne? Have you checked your messages?"

Suzanne fumbled her phone out of her back pocket.

She'd set it to silent when they began the investigation. She hit the power button with her thumb and the screen glowed, showing four missed calls from Gerry.

A new kind of horror drained all the remaining color from her face.

"Sit down, Suzanne. Sit down and I'll tell you what happened." Gerry guided her back to the chair in the parlor and guided her gently down.

And then he told his tale.

"Your brother – Mitch. He… Well, the sheriff came to the house, Suzanne. They – the sheriff's department – discovered his car about three miles outside of town. He'd gone off the road, crashed into a tree. The driver side door was open, the interior lights still on. It can't have happened that long ago. They followed a set of fading footsteps. It seems that he made it almost two miles, walking in the snow. And then he… well, they think he must have… have just gotten too cold to go on. He seems to have sat down against a tree, and just… just stopped, Suzanne. That's where they found him. He was frozen… he was dead, Suzanne," Gerry said.

"Mitch is dead."

Mitch

As he walked nearer to the incandescent figure in the hallway, the light which shone forth from it exploded around him in a welcoming warmth.

Pins and needles danced along the skin of his arms and face, and he relaxed into a comforting peace.

The light flared, enveloped him, and then he felt himself dissolving, floating upward.

There was no fear in his mind, no panic. He simply rose above it all.

Millie

Mitch's form became clearer as he walked toward her. Even the shadowy sentries on either side of the door didn't stop him.

He walked right through them as though they weren't there. Always brave, her boy.

Faced everything in life head on.

Her son walked into her arms, and she wrapped them around him, a thousand memories of his childhood skipping cheerfully through her mind; every scraped knee, hurt feeling, sob of frustration, comforted by his mother's embrace.

He was home now, her Mitch.

Home where he belonged.

Mitch

Mitch was surprised to open his eyes and find himself in his old bedroom.

He was, really, surprised to open his eyes at all. He felt the old familiar springs of his mattress beneath him, recognized at once each and every poster on the walls.

He frowned a bit at the sight of his old childhood toy, the robot he'd called Phantom, lying on its side in the middle of the floor.

That wasn't where it belonged.

In the doorway stood his mother.

He knew that couldn't be right. His mother. She couldn't be there. She… Was he losing his mind? Hallucinating? Dreaming?

He shivered suddenly, an icy chill seeping into him like water into a blanket.

He blinked his eyes as his vision was obscured by a thick, blinding whiteness, like… snow.

There was something about the snow, a world of white all around him, cold, painful at first then numbing, cold in his fingers and toes and then in his veins.

His body shook violently with unwanted recollection. He felt himself spiraling away in the cold oblivion.

A warm hand on his shoulder brought him back. He looked up into his mother's wrinkled face, shook his head to dislodge the feeling, half expecting snow to fall from his hair as he did.

His mother seemed real enough; the slight weight of her hand felt solid.

But as he gazed up at her, she seemed faded somehow, blurred around the edges. The look on her face frightened him, a look of love and concern that seemed to shout into his brain that something was very, very wrong.

She sat on the bed next to him, paused a few moments, staring off toward the wall as she gathered her thoughts.

"Mitch, my darling boy, I have something to tell you. I'm not sure, but I think…"

Her words were interrupted by another voice, a familiar voice which seemed to rush on a gust of wind up the stairs and circle the ceiling of Mitch's bedroom.

Both Mitch and his mother looked up, startled, at the sound, as if they thought they'd see the words themselves flying around the walls above them.

"Hello… anyone there? … me, Suzanne… show me you're here…"

The world dropped away.

The mattress dissolved to nothingness beneath him as his mouth formed around a silent word: *Suze?*

Mitch's body drifted, weightless, through the floor of his bedroom and into the dark shadowy recesses of the downstairs hallway.

Ahead of him, near the front door, stood a mass of huddled silhouettes. He took one step toward the door but jumped back quickly as a bright beam of light cut through the windows on either side of the door.

The door opened. Another shadowy figure.

Mitch strained to make out who or what it was, but something was wrong with his vision. All the moving shapes seemed like just that: shapes, out of focus.

A new shape emerged from the parlor, and though it was also dark and strange, Mitch could detect a slight difference: a halo, an aura of light shone around this one.

The face was obscured in gray shadow, but he knew the features of the silhouette, knew the height and the shape and the movement of his own sister.

"Suze!" he shouted, but she didn't turn, didn't react at all.

It was as if she couldn't hear him, and deep down in his gut a fear began to gnaw.

Mitch leaned his head against the wall and closed his eyes. Vertigo was setting in, a whirling vortex threatening to suck him down into its nothingness.

He listened.

He heard his own name. *Mitch.*

"Mitch is dead."

The gnawing grew, spread, infected his mind, his heart, his soul.

"No!" he shouted, a strangled, desperate sound.

He couldn't breathe, couldn't move, couldn't think. Cold bands of terror wrapped themselves around him, rooting him to the spot.

Mitch fell away, blinked out of consciousness and existence.

His mother watched him from above and sighed.

"Oh, Mitch."

CHAPTER TWENTY-ONE

Suzanne

The night she found out her brother was dead was one of the worst of her life.

She placed it somewhere at the top of the list, up there with the day of her abortion, and the moment she'd had to come, slinking and defeated, back to her mother's house afterward.

It was also, by far, the strangest, most surreal night of her life.

Three weeks later, as she lay in bed thinking it over, so much of it still felt impossible.

They'd broken up the investigation after Gerry arrived with the news, of course. Suzanne had ridden home with her husband, who had promptly given her a sleeping pill and tucked her warmly into bed.

The team had been left behind to pack their equipment and lock up.

Three days later, while the melting snow dripped from the eaves of the Hillview Baptist Church, they'd held Mitch's funeral.

Gerry had been wonderful, taking care of most of the arrangements while Suzanne sat, red-eyed, exhausted, drugged, doing her best to nod at the right times when the funeral director spoke to her.

The service was small.

Suzanne, and by extension Gerry, were the only family in attendance.

There were aunts and uncles and cousins, certainly, but they were scattered across the country, and no one really expected them to show up to a funeral a thousand miles away, in the snow, on Christmas Eve.

A few of Mitch's old high school buddies were there, looking embarrassed and awkward, and even a couple of their mother's ancient friends showed up and sat in the back row, dressed in full black mourning as if it were their own son who had passed away.

Suzanne thought of them now, the two old biddies. They had approached her after the service, the shorter one gripping Suzanne's hands tightly between her own.

"Sweet Suzie," she'd said, her voice a wavering croak, and Suzanne had grimaced at the use of the old nickname.

"So sad, my dear, so sad. But… your mother? She didn't come? Is she in a bad way, dear? I haven't spoken to her in so long."

Suzanne had swayed a little on the spot, Mitch's arm strong and steady around her waist keeping her upright. She had stared at the little old woman, who looked back up at her with innocence.

She must be senile, Suzanne thought, *dementia or Alzheimer's or something*. She forced herself to smile.

"Oh, I'm sorry, did you not know? My mother… she's been dead for three years now. She fell down the stairs to the basement when she went to look for a lightbulb."

The older woman's face registered horror, then confusion.

Her friend took her by the hand and pulled her away, patting her shoulders and whispering to her as they shuffled down the aisle.

Suzanne had looked at Gerry, and he had shrugged his shoulders.

The cemetery had been the hardest, a bitterness rising up in Suzanne as she stood by her brother's freshly dug grave. How many times had she come here to visit her mother? How many times had she sat and poured her heart out to a stone and a moldering body?

Mitch had never visited, not once. He had ignored their mother in life and in death, and yet still he had been her favorite.

Suzanne had gone home that day and taken another sleeping pill. She didn't like the thoughts that came into her mind when it was clear. Mitch. Her mother. The strange sights and sounds and feelings of that night in the old house. She had slept.

Suzanne knew she had to be clear minded for today, though, and so she hadn't taken a pill in the last forty-eight hours.

Thus, she was laying in her bed, staring at the curtains on her bedroom window as they swayed slightly in the hot air from the vent below.

Gerry had already gone to work, the look of worry that had creased his face for several days lightened a little at his wife's improved mental clarity. She supposed she had been a little out of it lately, sleeping most of the time and only barely coherent the rest.

But today… today she had places to go, people to see. Today she had her final meeting with the Hillview Paranormal Research Team.

When the bedside clock read nine, Suzanne pushed back the blankets and sat up. She went to the bathroom and started the shower, laying out warm clothes to dress in, and stepping out of the pajamas that had been her uniform for the last few weeks.

The water pelted down, hot and hard. Her skin turned red and steamed, just the way she liked it.

Suzanne lathered her body with soap, rinsed, and repeated the same with her hair. In the tiny, black hole world of the shower, she closed her eyes and let the thoughts she'd kept at bay come rushing back in.

The moment Gerry had broken the awful news.

The otherworldly glowing lights.

The snow falling heavy and thick as Gerry bundled her out to the waiting truck.

Her brother's body on the morgue table, cold and blue-tinged.

The mysterious thumps in the parlor.

The funeral, somber and sad.

The two old women, asking about her mother.

Oh, God, her mother. The day Suzanne had found her, three years ago, at the bottom of the basement steps.

Hot tears mixed with the water from the shower as Suzanne relived the memory. Her mother had been complaining about the light being out in the parlor.

Suzanne had told her she'd be by the next day, a Saturday, to replace it. She had warned her mother not to try to go down into the basement herself.

She had made a mental note to move all the spare bulbs up into the kitchen, because knowing her mother, she wouldn't listen, she'd just keep insisting on doing it herself.

And so Suzanne had arrived at her mother's house that Saturday morning. She had called for her mother, checked upstairs, felt a growing worry as each room revealed only dusty furniture and stale air.

She could see so clearly in her mind her own hand reaching out, opening the basement door – unlocked as it never should have been.

She could feel the rickety steps beneath her feet as she'd gone as quickly as she dared to the pile of clothes at the bottom of the stairs that was her mother.

Following the ambulance to the hospital.

Three days sitting by her mother's bedside, holding her small, limp hand and listening to the machines keeping her mother alive.

Waiting for her brother, who swore he'd come as soon as he was able, which was of course two days too late.

The one word her mother had uttered in her unconscious sleep, only one word in those three never-ending days: "Mitch."

Suzanne's own hot tears, angry and hurt and lonely.

Her mother's funeral, the numbness that set in then.

Coming home and standing at the doorway to the guest room they'd been fixing up for her mother to stay in. If she'd only hurried things along, gotten her mother moved in with her just one week earlier than planned… Suzanne had shut the door firmly, and it had stayed shut for three years, boxes of her mother's things stacked up against the walls, gathering dust.

Suzanne stepped forward into the hot stream of the shower, taking slow breaths and willing the water to wash away her pain, her grief, her guilt.

Suzanne's skin still held a warm pink glow when she stepped out the door of her front house and locked it behind her.

Gerry had expressed some concern at the thought of her driving, but she had assured him that after a couple of days without taking the pills, she'd be fine.

Besides, it was only a five-minute drive down to Main Street.

She pulled in outside the team's office and made her way carefully around drifts of dirty gray snow.

The door to the office was open again and Suzanne walked in.

The team, a moment before engaged in conversation, went silent at the sight of her. She tried to smile.

Melissa stood and came to her, putting an arm around her shoulder and guiding her to a chair at the table.

They didn't know what to say. Suzanne could see it on their faces. They thought she was fragile, some delicate glass thing that could break at the wrong word.

She smiled again, trying to reassure them – and herself, if she was being honest.

"Alright, I'm here," she said, her voice sounding surprisingly strong.

"What do you have to show me?"

Suzanne had been surprised, overwhelmed by the videos and the audio clips the team had shown her the first time she'd sat here in this room with them, but this time she was more ready, less surprised, though the things they showed her were even more extraordinary than before.

They started off with the things she had experienced herself. Temperature fluctuations, creaking stairs, amazingly blurry video of the ghostly lights.

"The spirits must have drained energy from our devices, causing them to glitch a bit," Jackson explained with an apologetic shrug.

And then they showed her the last video.

She was instructed to wear her headphones, because though it was video, video caught on the camera they had set up late in the investigation, in the corner by the front door, it wasn't so much the video that had them both excited and concerned.

It was the accompanying audio.

Suzanne stared intently at the monitor and listened.

There was chaos on the screen: Teresa, Melissa, Carrie, all huddled together, Gerry standing just inside the doorway, Suzanne staring at him as he spoke.

She didn't want to hear this part again, closed her eyes against the thought.

"Here, let me skip forward just a tiny bit," Jackson offered.

He did a bit of magic with the computer mouse and the sound started up again in her headphones.

The people were still on screen, but no one was speaking. Suzanne could hear her own recorded sobs, muffled against the front of Gerry's coat.

A sudden loud voice shouted into her ears, one long anguished wail of *Nooooooooo*, the tortuous pain and despair of the sound shooting through her like fire.

Suzanne gasped.

She pulled off the headphones and practically threw them onto the table.

She looked, wild-eyed and frantic, at the team assembled around her.

"No," she said.

She put her hands over her face and shook her head back and forth.

"No, no, no, no, no!"

It took a few minutes for her to calm down. The voice had unnerved her, its familiarity making it unmistakable. But there was more.

With soothing words and awkward pats, the team convinced her to put the headphones back on.

She closed her eyes, rested her head in her hands as she listened. The sound started, a faint static, then the gut-wrenching cry came again.

Suzanne stiffened against it, squeezed her eyes tight.

A moment passed.

Then, over the line, a whistling sigh like the wind through summer trees, and one more voice, doubly familiar, whispering two words through the headphones pressed to Suzanne's ears.

"Oh, Mitch."

CHAPTER TWENTY-TWO

Mitch stood by the window in his old bedroom.

It was snowing again. He'd never seen so much snow in one winter in his life. He laughed; scornful, broken. *In his life.*

Well, this wasn't life anymore, was it? He wasn't sure what it was. It certainly wasn't heaven. It was possible it was hell, stuck in his childhood home with his batty mother's ghost for all eternity.

Yes, that could be hell.

But he was trying to make the most of it.

His mother, having been dead a full three years longer than him, had mastered some abilities that he still had to work at.

It took concentration to keep from floating down through floors or up through ceilings. It took intense focus to touch and move things. It took a great stretch of the imagination to believe that the food his mother cooked in the kitchen was real, and even more imagination to think he'd even want to eat.

But his mother seemed to have settled into a routine, much like the one she'd had in her days of living. The only difference, it seemed, was that they both slept during daylight and rose back into consciousness as twilight fell.

Like bloody vampires.

Mitch laughed again at the thought. He then considered gravely how often he laughed at strange little things lately.

Was it possible to go crazy, *after* you died?

That would be an interesting thing to research. If only he had access to the internet! Well, there was the small library downstairs. His father's old psychiatry books were there, the ones that had sparked Mitch's own interest in the field as a young boy.

He supposed he could read through them all again. It wasn't as if he had any other pressing matters demanding his time.

Millie bustled about in the kitchen, making tea.

Mitch would be down soon, and they could have a nice cup before beginning their night together. She so enjoyed him being here. Having a man about the house made her feel safer.

And since he'd come home to take care of her, those nasty frightening shadows and strange disturbing knocks had disappeared completely.

Yes, she quite enjoyed having her son home.

Suzanne went through the boxes of her mother's things that summer.

Some things which her mother had insisted on packing went straight into the trash can. The rest went into a much smaller stack of boxes, and one July day, when the sun shone hot and bright and freezing cold snowy evenings were far from her mind, she loaded it all into her car and took it back up to the house on the hill.

No one had been inside since that night just before Christmas, and the dust was thicker than ever.

Suzanne caught the scent of fresh baked cookies as she stepped into the kitchen, and her mouth tweaked in a sad little smile.

OK, Mother, she thought, *enjoy your cookies, and you too, Mitch.*

A single tear started down her cheek, and she wiped it away angrily. She refused to cry anymore, she absolutely refused.

She tidied up the dishes on the counter and checked that the stove wasn't on.

She walked through the house room by room, thought about all the changes that could be made to make it more modern, knew that she'd never really change anything.

She laid back on the bed in her own room and dozed off for a bit, then went downstairs and sat in her mother's favorite chair to watch the sun set.

When the world turned to evening beyond the window, she picked up her purse, gave the chair a pat, and walked out the front door, locking it behind her.

She stood at her car gazing up at the house for a moment before she left and jumped when the drapes hanging over the window of her mother's bedroom window twitched.

"Just a draft," she told herself, though she knew it wasn't true.

Millie watched her daughter drive away down the hill into town.

Mitch stood behind her, sparkling ethereal tears running down his face. He didn't bother to wipe them away. Millie turned to her son, patted his wet cheek.

"Don't worry, my darling boy. Suzie will be back again. And one day… she'll come home for good, just like you did."

Mitch turned and walked away, down the stairs and into the office to read.

Millie lingered at the window a moment longer, then followed him down on her way to the kitchen to brew up some more tea.

CASE NOTES
PARANORMAL RESEARCH TEAM

CASE #04
HILLVIEW, MISSOURI

NOVEMBER 16 – DECEMBER 21, 2020

PARTICIPANTS: TERESA RUTLEDGE, JACKSON GREEN, CARRIE JAMESON, MELISSA NEWARK

BACKGROUND: House, built 1899. Two story Victorian plus basement and attic. Empty since 2017. Owned by Suzanne Carver-Bowles, daughter of last living resident, Millicent "Millie" Carver. Reports given by owner: noises (bumps, creaks, footsteps); objects appearing in a different place than left on previous visits; doors opening; lights coming on/going off by themselves; tampering with thermostat; disembodied voices; cold spots; feeling of presence on stairs.

INVESTIGATION:

NOVEMBER 16, 2020: Obtained permission from local owner, Suzanne Carver-Bowles, to enter and investigate house. Entered 5 pm to set up static cameras and familiarize with house layout. Electricity/water/gas still on in house for caretaker use. Base command set up in kitchen at rear, southwest corner of house. Notable findings: recorded cold spot, northwest corner of front parlor at 11:30 pm; recorded faint footsteps in downstairs hallway at 12:27 am; recorded stairs creaking 1:08 am; recorded physical thermostat setting change had occurred, 3:32 am (thermostat set to 66 degrees upon entrance, set to 74 degrees when checked again), thermostat is old/non-electronic/non-programmable; attempted EVP sessions 11:40 pm and 4:00 am, no response.

NOVEMBER 23, 2020: Second visit. Base command again in rear kitchen. Notable findings: recorded what seems to be music, located second floor, fading as we went closer 10:53 pm; recorded stairs creaking 11:26 pm; recorded cold spot in kitchen, near basement door, 12:03 am; attempted EVP session 12:12 am, no response; attempted communication via knocking, 1:00 am, possible faint knocks recorded; thermostat check revealed no change.

NOVEMBER 30, 2020: Third visit. First time investigating upstairs. Cold spot recorded on bed, left side, master bedroom, 10:16 pm; light coming on by itself and recorded faint humming sound (music?) southeast bedroom, 10:59 pm; attempted EVP session, master bedroom, 11:32 pm, no response; recorded stairs creaking, 11:52 pm;; attempted communication via knocking, kitchen, 12:30 am, no response; recorded shadow figure movement, downstairs hallway, 12:50 am; thermostat check recorded nine degree difference, 1:12 am; attempted second communication via knocking, front parlor, recorded knocking plainly heard with human ear, does not seem intelligent, knocks in random numbers instead of one for yes, two for no.

DECEMBER 7, 2020: Fourth visit. Immediately upon arrival, found kitchen in disarray. Cabinet doors open, several dishes and pans removed from cabinets and placed on counters. Oven turned on. Telekinesis? Also noticed a distinct smell permeating entire downstairs. Sweet like baked goods. Clairalience? Noted significant battery drain on all devices, Jackson procured new batteries from van, 11:46 pm; heard disembodied voice seeming to come from upstairs, 11:44 pm (heard by T, M, and C while J was outside, unfortunately with batteries dead in all recorders, this was heard by ear but not captured); upon investigating upstairs discovered a bedroom door that had been previously closed was now open, 11:52 pm; attempted gentle provocation using toy robot found on floor of northwest bedroom upstairs, with surprising results: a desk in the room began to shake and loud bumps were heard in the area, thermal scan indicated a cold spot in front of desk, temperature difference of eleven degrees, 12:28 am; attempted EVP session, later listening revealed what sounds like a woman's voice but no words are discernable, sounds almost like crying or whimpering, 12:56 am; attempted again to communicate via knocking, still in in northwest bedroom, in response bed seemed to shake, followed by loud but slow rhythmic thumping, similar to footsteps but very muted, 1:30 am. After this all activity, which had been so promising, stopped abruptly.

DECEMBER 14, 2020: Fifth visit. Recorded footsteps in downstairs hallway, 10:08 pm; recorded kitchen table – covered in equipment – first shaking and then sliding across floor – major telekinetic phenomena!, 10:36 pm; recorded shadow figure near table, seen with naked eye and recorded with handheld cam, 10:42 pm; recorded major cold spot near table which then moved to surround Jackson in his seat at table, temperature drop of ten degrees, lasting twelve (!) minutes, physically noticeable by Jackson, who was visibly shivering by the end, 10:46-10:58 pm; attempted communication via knocking while monitoring cold spot, received several varied knockings emanating from near the cold spot, no discernable pattern or seeming intelligent responses to questions, 10:48-10:58 pm; attempted EVP session, asking standard questions to identify presence, upon asking what the spirit's name was an audible voice was heard, upon playback voice clearly says the name "Arthur", 11:05 pm; recorded basement door visibly and audibly shaking, then opening and closing once, 11:12 pm; attempted communication via knocking, no response, 11:18 pm; recorded sounds heard from basement, indistinct bumps, 11:23 pm; no more activity was recorded this night but note that thermostat had been shifted by nine degrees again between beginning and end of investigation, 11:58 pm.

DECEMBER 21, 2020: Recorded master bedroom door moving, 9:07 pm; recorded temperature change, cold spot surrounding home owner Carver-Bowles, 9:11 pm; recorded front door opening by itself, 9:31 pm, attempted debunking, results inconclusive; recorded spirit orb in parlor, 9:45 pm; recorded muffled knocks followed by items on mantle shaking, front parlor, 10:12 pm; recorded spirit orb in parlor moving toward second light in hallway, bright flash of white light upon the meeting of the two lights, 10:20 pm; (here the investigation was interrupted by the arrival of homeowner's husband, investigation terminated in light of news, upon reviewing footage the next day, one final EVP was found on the downstairs hall camera: a male voice cries out clearly the word, "NO", all members agree the voice sounds as if it is in pain, this voice is followed 42 seconds later by a rushing sound, like a loud sigh, and two whispered words, which sound like, "Oh, Mitch."

CONCLUSION: the HPRT believes this house to be the location of true spirit activity. Shadow figures, knockings, orbs, and voice phenomena reveal this to be true. The owner, Suzanne Carver-Bowles has chosen not to pursue any further investigations into the house.

H.D. Daughrity loves all things macabre, ghoulish, witchy, dark, and horrific. She lives with her husband, her extended circus of children and pets, and more books than any one house can hold, split between the East Coast, and her native state of Oklahoma, where she spends her days writing, editing, gardening, and keeping heads in the clouds, and feet on the ground.

Visit H.D. Daughrity for news, to purchase her books, writings, see her appearances, peruse her professional book reviews, and contact her for editing services at *www.heathermillerhorror.com*.

This work of fiction was formatted using 12-point Times New Roman Font, on 60lb cream stock paper. The page size is 5.06" x 7.81." The margins are industry standard 0.8" for top, bottom, and 0.25" outside. There is no inside margin but has 0.63" mirrored gutters with no bleed. The cover is full color Trade Paperback in a glossy finish. The binding is 'perfect.'